She wanted him as a woman wants a man

Commander Stevens stood more than six feet tall, with wavy brown hair and hazel eyes that changed with his thoughts. In his pristine white uniform, he stirred emotions in her that no other man had managed to stir.

May had promised herself she would never let a man control her again. Certainly not a person from another country. She'd spent her life as a member of the Baronovian royal family, with a position to be upheld. Upholding that position often kept her from going where her heart and her interests led her.

Now, to her surprise, her heart had led her straight to a man she could never make her own.

Dear Reader,

Welcome to Harlequin American Romance, where you're guaranteed heartwarming, emotional and deeply romantic stories set in the backyards, big cities and wide-open spaces of America. Kick starting the month is Cathy Gillen Thacker's *Her Bachelor Challenge*, which launches her brand-new family-connected miniseries THE DEVERAUX LEGACY. In this wonderful story, a night of passion between old acquaintances has a sought-after playboy businessman questioning his bachelor status.

Next, Mollie Molay premieres her new GROOMS IN UNIFORM miniseries. In *The Duchess & Her Bodyguard*, protecting a royal beauty was easy for a by-the-book bodyguard, but falling in love wasn't part of the plan! Don't miss *Husbands, Husbands…Everywhere!* by Sharon Swan, in which a lovely B & B owner's ex-husband shows up on her doorstep with amnesia, giving her the chance to rediscover the man he'd once been. This poignant reunion romance story is the latest installment in the WELCOME TO HARMONY miniseries. Laura Marie Altom makes her Harlequin American Romance debut with *Blind Luck Bride*, which pairs a jilted groom with a pregnant heroine in a marriage meant to satisfy the terms of a bet.

This month, and every month, come home to Harlequin American Romance—and enjoy!

Best,

Melissa Jeglinski
Associate Senior Editor
Harlequin American Romance

THE DUCHESS
& HER BODYGUARD
Mollie Molay

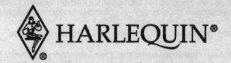

HARLEQUIN®

TORONTO • NEW YORK • LONDON
AMSTERDAM • PARIS • SYDNEY • HAMBURG
STOCKHOLM • ATHENS • TOKYO • MILAN • MADRID
PRAGUE • WARSAW • BUDAPEST • AUCKLAND

For Hudson Thomas Fox.
Welcome to the world.

ISBN 0-373-16938-8

THE DUCHESS & HER BODYGUARD

ABOUT THE AUTHOR

After working for a number of years as a logistics contract administrator in the aircraft industry, Mollie Molay turned to a career she found far more satisfying—writing romance novels. Mollie lives in Northridge, CA, surrounded by her two daughters and eight grandchildren, many of whom find their way into her books. She enjoys hearing from her readers and welcomes comments. You can write to her at Harlequin Books, 300 East 42nd St., 6th Floor, New York, NY 10017.

Books by Mollie Molay

HARLEQUIN AMERICAN ROMANCE

Special Invitation

Commander Wade Stevens
Judge Advocate General Corps
Department of the Navy

You are cordially invited to attend
the State Department reception in honor of

Prince Alexis of Baronovia
and his daughter
Duchess Mary Louise

at Blair House
1631 Pennsylvania Avenue

Formal attire required

Prologue

Wade Stevens felt someone's intent gaze boring into the back of his head. A practicing lawyer, he was used to being the focus of attention, but tonight felt different. Tonight, the vibrations reaching him were making the hair on the back of his neck stand on end.

After all, he wasn't in court, he told himself as he glanced around him for the offender. He was attending a diplomatic cocktail party as the representative of the Navy's Judge Advocate General Corps, more commonly known as JAG. In his white dress uniform, surely he was no different from the variety of uniformed men in attendance.

Casually, he rubbed the back of his neck. And, just as casually, slowly turned to survey the activity going on around him.

The parlor of Blair House across the street from the White House and currently the temporary residence of Prince Alexis of Baronovia, and his daughter, the duchess Mary Louise, was ablaze with lights. The buzz of conversation almost drowned out the soft music played by a quintet of uniformed U.S. Marine musicians. The air was filled with the appetizing scent of hors d'oeuvres being offered by white-gloved waiters. Foreign notables from countries around Europe were easily identified by the multitude of colorful ribbons and medals on their chests. United States diplomats were equally distinguishable by their conservative tuxedoes. Wade's experienced gaze didn't miss the men in suits, CIA and FBI operatives, who attempted to fade into the woodwork.

The women guests in attendance outshone each other in obligatory little black cocktail dresses or in the currently popular red version. More than one woman wore strands of colorful jewels at her neck, wrists and in her hair.

With the exception of one exquisite woman.

A woman who drew Wade's gaze as surely as slivers of steel are drawn to a magnet.

She wore a flowing white chiffon dress, which, although gracefully draped over her breasts, managed to reveal more of her shapely figure than it concealed. When his gaze threatened to linger there, he caught himself and moved on to the rest of her. Her short skirt ended in a swirl of sheer material just above her knees. Long and slender legs were covered in shimmering silk hose and she wore white satin sandals with four-inch heels.

Without a doubt, Wade mused, the lady in white was the most attractive woman he'd seen in too long a time.

Fascinated, he gazed at rich chestnut-brown hair drawn back from her forehead into a chignon that rested on the nape of her neck. Soft tendrils had escaped their bounds to hang temptingly over her forehead. An emerald necklace that matched her eyes circled a slender neck his fingers instinctively ached to caress. If only, he told himself, he could find out for himself if her skin was as silky as it appeared to be.

Their eyes met. A warmth covered him when she gazed back at him over the rim of the flute of champagne she held to her lips. To his chagrin, she smiled, and her exotic eyes sparkled with subtle understanding at his obvious interest. With a slight smile and a nod, she saluted him with the flute of champagne.

When he noted a mutual interest reflected in those emerald-green eyes, Wade ran his finger under his suddenly tight uniform collar. He was debating joining her and introducing himself when she turned away to speak to a dignitary who appeared at her side.

Wade gave a resigned shrug. As beautiful as she was, a woman like her was bound to be taken. Too bad. Still, there was no mistaking the gleam of interest he'd seen in her eyes.

An hour later, when he was engaged in a sedate waltz with the wife of the undersecretary of the navy, he saw the woman in white glance at him from across the room. Again he noticed those green eyes and that impossible smile that kicked his heart into high gear. Then she was gone.

A small voice whispering inside his head told him it was going to be a memorable night.

Chapter One

"You've got to be kidding!" Wade said.

He stared at the man who, moments before, had tapped him on his shoulder and invited him into the quiet, well-stocked library of the Blair House. As he was an avid lover of books, a setting like this normally would have attracted his interest. Not tonight.

At the frown that came over the undersecretary of the navy's forehead, Wade straightened and crisply added, "Sir."

Undersecretary Peter Logan acknowledged the formal address with a curt nod. "No, Commander. I assure you I'm not kidding. In fact, I've never been more serious. I've just asked you to escort Duchess Mary Louise of Baronovia for the remainder of her visit here in Washington."

"Why me?" Wade ventured. He'd gone through the academy, basic training and graduate school to become a lawyer. Acting as an escort in performance of his duties wasn't his idea of serving his country.

"With due respect, sir, I'm a lawyer," he said cautiously. "You of all people should know our reputation. How interesting would I be as an escort?"

"That depends on you," Logan said with a fleeting smile. "I seem to recall you had some bodyguard training and that you've been assigned to escort duty before this. In fact, the way I understood it, Commander, you were more than an escort. You were actually a bodyguard."

Wade cleared his throat at the reminder. His brief stint as a bodyguard had almost taken ten years off his life, and he wasn't anxious to duplicate the drill. "That was to protect a witness in a court case, sir. And if you remember," he added with a wry smile, "I almost lost the poor woman in the process."

"I remember." Logan's lips curved in a calculating way that made Wade's mental antennae rise like a rocket and his spirits sink just as fast. "However, Commander," Logan went on, "I'm sure the experience has made you aware of the importance of never taking your eyes off your charge. Am I correct?"

Wade nodded reluctantly and, from the look on Logan's face, had a feeling somehow he was in for a surprise. This request that he act as an escort to the duchess wasn't the whole story. He took a deep breath. "Why don't you tell me something about the lady?"

Logan smiled, and a twinkle came into his eyes. "The duchess is Prince Alexis's young daughter."

Wade blinked. Raised with three younger brothers, he knew zip about little girls, and even less on how to entertain them. Outside of the well-known Children's Museum, the National Zoo and the Doll House and Toy Museum in D.C., he would be hard put to come up with places to take her. The prospect of escorting and entertaining the little duchess around D.C. blew his mind. He'd be the laughingstock of the JAG Corps.

"His young daughter? I'm afraid you've picked the wrong person for the job, sir. Sounds to me you need a nursemaid or a nanny..."

Logan guffawed until tears came into his eyes. When he was finally able to control himself, he gasped. "Maybe I should brief you a little before I introduce you to the duchess." He gestured to a large wine-colored leather chair. "Have a seat."

Resigned to the inevitable, Wade sank into the chair. At the same time he wished he'd thought to pick up another flute of champagne to see him through the briefing.

Logan sank into a seat and leaned forward. "To be brief and to the point," he began, "the Prince of Baronovia is here at the request of the State Department. To the public, the reason the prince, his daughter and his entourage are housed in the Blair House is that Baronovia is too small a country to have its own embassy here in Washington. The actual reason they are staying in the Blair House is somewhat more delicate and confidential.''

Wade shifted uncomfortably in his chair. He was beginning to sense there was more to the scenario than Logan was willing to admit. Especially when Logan had already mentioned ''bodyguard'' in the same breath as ''escort.''

''And?''

''For now, that's all I can tell you,'' Logan went on. ''Suffice it to say the department is very interested in keeping the prince and the duchess happy and safe during their stay. When the duchess specifically requested you to escort her while her father attends to affairs of state, we all agreed you were the perfect solution to keeping her happy.''

''Why me? I don't even know her.''

''Because we also know she'll be safe with you.''

Safe? Wade straightened up and turned all of his attention on Logan. If he was expected to participate in what sounded like more than just simple affairs of state, he intended to learn more of the facts. ''If Baronovia is such a small country, why would the State Department be so interested in it? Let alone worried about the safety of its ruler?''

Logan glanced around the room as if to make sure they were alone, then lowered his voice. "Until now we've only had a trade mission in Baronovia. With all the unrest in the area, we decided it was time to upgrade the mission to an embassy with U.S. Marines to guard it. The State Department is hoping to persuade the prince to sign a treaty agreement that will allow us to do so."

Wade frowned as the facts began to sink in. This wasn't going to be a run-of-the-mill assignment, not if there were significant political overtones. There had to be more to the story than the secretary was admitting. It was time to find out. "Go on."

Logan paced the library, paused to consider Wade and finally appeared to make up his mind. "Just between you and me, Commander, the personnel we intend to station in Baronovia will also act as the eyes and ears of our State Department—an arrangement a few of the smaller countries surrounding Baronovia strongly oppose. Our presence in the area isn't very popular at the present time. Unfriendly elements in the region might seek to discourage our plans by attempting to disrupt the prince's visit. Of course," he added in a confidential voice, "I don't expect you to share this information with anyone."

Wade sank back into the leather chair. The last thing he needed at this stage of his life was a kid who might be in trouble. Or a country that could be incinerated at any given moment. "Just what are my chances of keeping the duchess out of trouble?"

"That's up to you, Commander. Of course, you'll have the backup of the Secret Service, but up-front you'll be her escort. We want to keep the duchess happy. Now don't get me wrong," Logan went on, "the responsibility for the duchess's safety and happiness is largely going to be up to you. Under the circumstances, I expect you to give yourself fully over to this assignment. This time," he cautioned dryly as he rose to his feet, "you will not, I repeat, will not lose your charge. Understood?"

The briefing obviously over, Wade rose to his feet. He wasn't too clear as to why a JAG lawyer was needed as an escort/bodyguard, but if the undersecretary of the navy was giving him orders he must have had the judge advocate general's concurrence. "Understood, sir."

Logan relaxed and shot him a conspiratorial smile that left Wade bewildered. "Then come with me. I'll introduce you to your charge."

When the grandfather clock in the corner struck eleven, Wade glanced at his watch. "Kind of past her bedtime, isn't it?"

Logan choked back a laugh. "Commander," he said jovially, "brace yourself. I think you're in for a surprise."

With Logan's laugh ringing in his ears, Wade reluctantly gave up the possibility that, given enough time, he might have connected with the lady in white sometime during the party.

Logan led him back to the party and, to Wade's bewilderment, straight to the side of the lady in white. At that point, the surprise Logan had promised him became the understatement of the year. Instead of acting as the escort of an innocent young girl as he'd been led to believe, his charge was the lady with the invitation in her exotic green eyes.

He took a deep breath and promised himself Undersecretary Logan hadn't heard the last of this. A joke was a joke, but this was too much. And he wasn't laughing.

Logan ignored Wade's pointed look. ''Your Grace, I'd like to introduce you to Commander Wade Stevens. As you requested, the commander will be your escort for the duration of your stay here in Washington. Commander, may I present Duchess Mary Louise of Baronovia.''

As requested?

Wade's head swam as he acknowledged the introduction. Requested by whom? The lady in white herself?

He hadn't set eyes on the duchess before tonight. And, outside of smiling at him over the rim of her flute of champagne, she hadn't paid any real attention to him. There had to be a mistake, and one he would remedy the first chance he got.

"Delighted to meet you, Commander Stevens," the duchess replied with a mischievous smile. She held out her hand. "I am looking forward to having you as my escort during my stay in your beautiful city."

Wade glanced at the two Secret Service men hovering behind the duchess and eyeing him as if he were a suspect. Like it or not, he had to keep his questions for a later time when he and the duchess had more privacy. "Looks as if we're going to be quite a cozy group," he commented dryly.

After a glance over her shoulder, the duchess frowned. "As long as I have you as my escort, Commander, I'm sure I will not be needing anyone else." She waved her hand in dismissal at the Secret Service men.

To give the men credit, they glanced at Wade and remained where they were.

Wade froze at her gesture. The sensuous duchess might have caught his attention, but her imperious royal manner was rapidly turning him off. It was time to make one thing clear: if he was going to be her escort, he intended to be in charge.

He gazed at her silently. Considering her age and her appearance, the Children's Zoo was out. And along with it any other diversions intended for children.

"You won't be needing the Secret Service?" he asked softly. When she shook her head, he turned to Undersecretary Logan. "This isn't going to work, sir. Secret Service assistance is part of the package or the deal is off."

Logan cleared his throat. "Excuse me, Your Grace, I'd like to have a moment with Commander Stevens." At her cool nod, he drew Wade aside. "We have no choice in the matter, Commander. The request for your services came through Prince Alexis himself and has been sanctioned by everyone, with the possible exception of the president. I'll see what I can do about making the Secret Service less conspicuous and more acceptable to the duchess, but I agree with you. They must remain."

Logan turned back to the duchess and said apologetically, "The commander is right, Your Grace. There's too much at stake here for you to go around D.C. without adequate protection. But I promise we will try to keep them in the background."

The duchess handed her empty champagne flute to a passing waiter with an expression that confirmed Wade's opinion of the lady. She *was* every bit as willful as she was beautiful.

"I want to see your beautiful city as an ordinary tourist," she said with a smile clearly intended to charm the socks off of Logan, but wasn't doing much for him. "I can hardly do it with an entourage. I'm sure the commander's presence will be sufficient to protect me." She patted Wade on his arm. "Right, Commander?"

Wade smothered a groan. It was bad enough that the duchess wasn't the young girl he'd been led to believe. Children could be put in their place, but this was no child. The very adult duchess was a spoiled woman whose tempting lips and flashing eyes were set on charming him into going along with whatever she wanted.

Fortunately, he was experienced enough as a man and as a lawyer to know that when a woman uses her charms to get her way there's bound to be trouble ahead. The trick was to stay one step ahead of the lady before she caused an international incident.

Bottom line, he sensed as he gazed down at her, was that her care and protection, with or without the Secret Service to back him up, promised to be a handful.

He glanced at the sculptured feminine hand that now clung to his arm. All his instincts to take advantage of the closeness she seemed to offer stirred, then died a quick death. He wasn't a lawyer for nothing. Her smile was an act.

In his ten years with the Judge Advocate General Corps, he'd persuaded many a jury to see his side of a case before the court. This case was no different. Sooner or later he and the duchess were going to have to come to an agreement about the Secret Service, or his name wasn't Wade Stevens. But not here in front of roomful of people. There was no point in creating a public spectacle of himself.

"Perhaps the duchess and I ought to have this discussion in private. Come to some sort of mutual understanding," he quietly said to Logan. When Logan nodded, Wade motioned to the Secret Service men to hold off while he straightened out his charge. "Your Grace, please come with me."

He offered his arm to the duchess and walked her to the library door. Before she could speak, he had led her into the library he'd left just moments before.

"Now see here, Your Grace," he began as soon as the door closed behind him. "I don't want to appear arbitrary, but there are some rules attached to the game we seem to be playing. Whether you like it or not."

"Game?" The duchess wandered over to a floor-to-ceiling bookcase, drew out a leather-bound book and casually turned the pages. "I do not know what you're talking about."

"With due respect, Your Grace, I think you do," Wade answered. "For starters, if you don't mind the plain language, you're going to have to knock off the royal act and come down off your high horse. If you're serious about seeing D.C. as a tourist, fine. But you're going to have to play strictly by the rules. My rules. The first of which is cooperating with the Secret Service. And," he added grimly, "you might as well cut out the siren act to get your way. It isn't going to work on me."

The duchess thrust the book back on the shelf and turned to face Wade. Gold sparks of anger shot through her eyes. "Anything else, Commander?"

"Yes," he said. "You're going to have to stop acting like a duchess and more like a tourist from New Jersey."

"But I *am* a duchess!"

"Maybe so, but with your regal bearing and custom-made clothing, no way in heaven are you going to pass for a typical tourist." Nor like an ordinary woman, he added silently. Not with those green eyes and chestnut hair and a body sure to draw second glances.

He expected the duchess to protest. To use her royal status as an excuse to overrule this bodyguard-as-an-escort business. To his surprise she stared at him for a few moments before she bit her lip and spoke up.

"And how do you propose to change me into a typical tourist, Commander?"

He was a dead man.

Contrary to his hopeful expectations, instead of

firing him, Duchess Mary Louise of Baronovia was actually going to go along with him! Grudgingly he had to give her credit. She'd not only gotten him for a bodyguard, she was smart. Smart enough to know when to fold.

All the more reason he had to be on his guard.

"First, Your Grace," he said eyeing her cocktail dress frankly, "we're going to go to Wal-Mart in the morning and outfit you in ordinary clothing."

Ordinary clothing to turn her into an ordinary woman? he asked himself as he continued to lay down the rules. No way! Clearly he was out of his mind for even thinking so. No matter what she wore or how she looked, the duchess Mary Louise could never be ordinary. Still, if it was the only way he could get her attention it was worth a try.

After a moment's pause, she shrugged. "You may be right. If you think clothing will make a difference, I'm willing. What else?"

"The Secret Service stays, both of them."

A blush rose over her face, and for a moment she almost looked human. "They are two old married men with old-fashioned minds. Everything I told them I wanted to see was off-limits."

Wade's sixth sense sounded warning signals. As in any big city, there were enough off-limit places in D.C. to blow any bodyguard-cum-escort's mind, and he was no different. Still, with him keeping an extra watchful eye on her and the two Secret Service men as backup, how much trouble could she get into?

"What exactly do you have in mind to see?"

"I'll let you know in the morning," she said airily and started to turn away.

"I don't play games, Your Grace, and neither should you." Wade said quietly. "To begin with, why don't you make a list of the places you'd like to visit. I'll look them over and let you know which ones I think are okay."

She stopped in her tracks, and her eyes narrowed. Without saying a word, Wade knew that under that cool facade she was angry…and that he didn't care. He was going to do his duty as he saw it, even if she didn't like it. Furthermore, he sensed she hadn't chosen him for an escort merely because he was younger than the Secret Service men assigned her. Age had nothing to do with it; she had to have another motive.

He raised his eyebrows and swallowed a begrudging smile. The angrier the duchess became, the more enchanting she looked, more the pity. For all her attraction, she could have come from another planet and was just as unreachable.

She didn't fool him, either. She may have agreed to dressing down, but strong-minded women like her never gave up, any more than a leopard could change its spots. It would only be a matter of time before the lady was back trying to use her wiles to persuade him to see things her way.

Thank God he was going to be hers only for a few days.

"If you don't mind my saying so, it sounds to me as if you've already tried your wiles on the Secret Service men and couldn't get away with it," he said dryly. "You can forget trying anything on me."

"Now see here, Commander," she retorted, all traces of the wistful and sexy woman gone in the blink of an eyelid. The imperious duchess was back. "In spite of what you think about me, I am not a spoiled child. Nor am I a fool. I am not looking for trouble, either. I merely wish to see your country's capital and I wish to see it my way."

"I don't have a problem with that as long as the Secret Service tags along," he agreed. And then he asked the question that continued to bother him. "Of all the men you could have asked for as an escort, why me?"

She looked at him cooly. "Simply put, Commander, I chose you for an escort because you looked to have an open mind and apparently knew how to enjoy yourself. So, if you think my dressing up or dressing down will make me inconspicuous, I will allow it."

Wade reluctantly nodded his agreement. In his

book the lady could never be inconspicuous. He might take her shopping for nondescript clothing, but as for her fading into the tourist landscape, he wasn't going to bank on it. Any more than he could bank on her complete cooperation.

To make matters worse, there seemed to be no way out of the escort duty.

Escorting the duchess around Washington might actually turn out to be interesting, he mused as he eyed the folds of sheer material designed to hide her pert breasts. Instead, they only managed to heighten his interest. He'd always felt that when a woman left some hint of modesty in her clothing, it did more for him than a blatant invitation.

Whoever had designed the duchess's cocktail dress had known exactly what he or she was doing. And, from his own reaction to the way she looked, he wouldn't have been surprised if the lady knew it, too. To muddy the waters, he was sure, from the parting look she gave him she hadn't given up on persuading him to see things her way.

He followed her back to the party with a sinking feeling in his middle. He was going to have to protect the lady for a few days. But who was going to protect him from her?

Chapter Two

She hadn't told him the whole truth.

May, as the family called her, hastily adjusted the neckline of the white evening dress that had drawn Wade Stevens's frankly interested gaze. The whole truth, a truth she wasn't about to share with him, was that she'd requested him as her escort because she'd been as attracted to him as he seemed to have been drawn to her.

His age, his personality and the probability he was more likely to understand her than the two older Secret Service men hovering over her, *had* been a factor in his favor. But the truth was that it had been his virile appearance in his immaculate white dress uniform that had first captivated her and then held her attention.

She'd kept her eyes on him while he'd worked his way through the room, occasionally stopping to chat with someone he knew. It had been his easy smile, the way the corner of his eyes crinkled as he laughed that had finally convinced her.

She'd sensed then he was a man who had a sense of humor and knew how to enjoy life. A man who would know how to make her laugh.

She hadn't known much laughter during her arranged marriage. Married at nineteen to a titled cousin, chosen for her by her father, she had tried to be the proper wife her late, older husband had expected. He had suddenly fallen dead at her feet of a heart attack a year ago.

Her period of mourning over, she had taken her father up on his invitation to travel with him on this short trip to the United States. She was desperate to enjoy her stay. Now was her chance to enjoy her youth and taste the freedom that had evaded her as a member of the royal family of Baronovia, and, until the recent birth of her half brother, its heir apparent.

The sight-seeing agenda laid out for her by the U.S. State Department had left her cold. The rules laid down by her Secret Service escorts had left her even colder. As for the commander, he may have been right about her wanting to see a side of Washington that was more than its stone monuments, but she didn't care. She was more determined than ever to visit the places she'd longed to see.

If it meant using her royal status to charm or intimidate him into seeing things her way, so be it.

It was too bad she had to play a game with him, she thought regretfully as he held the door open for her. He appeared to be a genuinely decent man. Just as she knew herself to be a flesh-and-blood human woman under the role of imperious royalty she was playing. In different circumstances she might have enjoyed meeting him.

"EVERYTHING SETTLED?" Undersecretary of the navy Logan materialized at Wade's elbow.

"You might say so, sir," Wade agreed cautiously with a glance at the duchess.

"Good." As Logan shook Wade's hand, his relief was evident. "What's on your sight-seeing agenda for tomorrow?"

"Sorry, sir," Wade replied. "I've found it best never reveal my plans ahead of time."

Logan started to speak, then appeared to change his mind. "Of course, Commander. You're in charge." He smiled at the duchess. "With your permission, Your Grace, I'll leave you in the commander's capable hands. Let me know if there's anything else I can do for you." He bowed and hurried away.

Wade had been tempted to laugh when Logan acted if a diplomatic crisis had been averted. A stickler for propriety and rules, if Logan had known of Wade's plans, he would have nixed the idea of shopping for appropriate clothing in Wal-Mart.

Somehow the idea didn't sound amusing anymore.

Wade gazed down at the duchess. She'd tried to use her charm on him to get her way, but it wasn't going to work. He'd actually expected her to tell Logan she'd changed her mind about wanting him for an escort. Instead, she'd slipped her hand through his arm, smiled and gazed up at Wade as if she was a star-struck fan of his.

Wade knew better. The wily duchess had an agenda. Although she seemed to have given in to his conditions for their outings, her teasing smile was a dead giveaway. Instinct told him the dimples that danced across her cheeks hid the truth.

He gazed down at her manicured hand. Another gesture that gave her away. He knew that royalty didn't normally touch strangers. The duchess was acting, trying to use charm to get her way. Only time and his watchful eyes would tell what was behind that smile of hers.

He didn't trust her as far as the front door to the Blair House.

''You *are* going to at least consult with me on our agenda, are you not?'' the duchess said in a silky voice that dripped with honey.

He wasn't buying.

Wade hesitated long enough to see her squirm, a question in her eyes. Good. He intended to keep her on edge while he laid down the rules. "That depends on what you have in mind."

She took her hand away. "To begin with, I saw all of your national monuments that I care to see on our way in from the airport. Now I want to see the other side of the city."

"Hold it right there," Wade ordered before the last words were out of her mouth. "I don't know what you mean by the other side of the city, but I have a strong suspicion it's the wrong side."

"Perhaps," she added with a frown. "At least, the Secret Service agents seemed to think so. Nevertheless I have my mind made up. I will see no more monuments."

"Really." Wade's eyebrows rose and came together. "Just what *did* you have in mind?"

"I shall give you a list tomorrow, after you call off the Secret Service. Right now I would like to speak to my father." She started to move away.

"As a matter of fact, so would I." Before she could take a second step, Wade touched her elbow and urged her to a corner of the room. "First let's get something straight, Your Grace. You tell me what you'd like to see, then I'll tell you if I agree.

And as for the Secret Service men, forget calling them off. Like I said, they're in.''

Her face paled and her eyes turned as cold as the glittering emeralds around her neck. ''I think you're forgetting who I am and who you are, Commander.''

Wade felt as if he'd been slapped in the face.

''Not at all, Your Grace,'' he said with as much restraint as he could muster. ''I'm Commander Wade Stevens, of the United States Navy. A lawyer attached to the Judge Advocate General Corps. While I'm not normally in the escort business, I am also the man you apparently asked for as an escort. And as your chosen escort I get to make the rules. You might say,'' he added dryly, ''you're in my hands for the duration of your stay.''

At the annoyed expression that came across her face, Wade began to wonder if the duchess actually knew the reason his government was interested in protecting her. Or if she realized that if she hadn't been in some kind of danger, the Secret Service and his own services would never have been called into play. Just how urgent remained to be seen.

He settled for the middle ground. ''Where I come from, Your Grace, anything worth doing is worth doing well. Especially after an order from my superiors. So, how about starting over? As long as we appear to be stuck with each other for the next few days, how about a truce?''

He knew, even as he asked the question, that any truce the lady might agree to wasn't going to be worth the powder to blow it to hell.

MAY GAZED in stony silence at the man who was turning out to be her bodyguard as well as her escort. Instead of being intimidated by her royal status, he appeared not to be impressed. Part of her was annoyed, even angry at his take-charge attitude. Another part, the sensible part of her, admired his courage. If there ever was a man she wanted as an escort around Washington, D.C., it was this Wade Stevens. From the moment she'd watched him make his way across the room in his eye-catching uniform, she'd sensed that a woman could be a woman and enjoy herself with him. Now, if she could only make him see things her way.

He stood more than six foot tall, with wavy brown hair and hazel eyes that changed with his thoughts. In his pristine white uniform, his athletic figure stirred emotions in her no other man before him had managed to do. Certainly not her late husband.

When their gazes locked, she realized that she wanted more than Wade Stevens's company. She wanted him as a woman wants a man, and, heaven forgive her, in ways she was almost embarrassed to contemplate.

On the other hand, attracted to him or not, she

had promised herself she would never let a man control her again the way her late husband had been wont to do. And certainly not a person from another country. Asking her to cooperate with him was one thing. Ordering her to do it was another.

She'd spent her life as a member of the Baronovian royal family, with a position to be upheld. Unfortunately, upholding that position had too often kept her from going where her heart and her interests had led her.

And now, to her surprise, her heart had led her straight to a man she could never make her own.

She had hoped things would be different in the United States, a country where her tutors had told her everyone had been created equal and everyone was free. Somewhere she could be herself—May Baron—instead of the Dowager Duchess Mary Louise.

If only she could tell him she wasn't the woman she appeared to be.

She pulled her thoughts together, told herself to ignore Wade, to ignore her attraction to him. She wanted to see how ordinary people lived in the United States, a country that had intrigued her for years. No way was she going home without seeing the city she'd read about in a magazine during her flight here.

Even though she came only to his chin, she drew

herself up to her full height. Instead of being May, the woman she actually yearned to be, she assumed the persona of Dowager Duchess Mary Louise of Lorrania, widow of the late duke of Lorrania. "I am going to speak to my father," she repeated. "And, since I am surely safe here, you may consider yourself at liberty to leave. I will see you at nine o'clock tomorrow morning."

Wade stared at her for tense moment before he shook his head and kept a studied smile on his face for the benefit of possible watchers. She'd agreed to go along with him a moment ago. What had changed her mind?

"Take it easy, Your Grace," he said. "*We'll* visit your father together. *Then,* I'll leave."

Prince Alexis paused in conversation with a foreign diplomat and greeted his daughter with a broad smile. "Ah, my dear, I was beginning to wonder where you were." He glanced at Wade as if he didn't know who he was. "Why don't you introduce your escort, my dear?"

Wade bit back a comment. According to Logan, the prince had been consulted about his daughter's choice of escort. Now, the prince was pretending not to know him. And not to know the duty included being his daughter's bodyguard as well as her escort. If the assignment was a secret, there had to be more here than met the eye. Hopefully, he thought with crossed fingers, an escort was all he would be called upon to be.

"Commander Wade Stevens of the United States Navy," Mary Louise replied distantly. "My father, Prince Alexis."

Wade shook the prince's hand. After seeing the fond gaze the man sent his daughter, Wade didn't have the heart to suggest his daughter needed to be told to listen to reason. Or to even suggest it was time to tell her all the reasons for their visit and any danger that might be attached to it.

"I just wanted to say good-night, Your Highness," Wade said after noting the wary look in the duchess's eyes. He knew, without her saying so, she wasn't anxious for her father to hear about her behavior. "With your permission, sir, I expect to pick up Her Grace tomorrow morning at nine."

"Of course, Commander. I'm sure my daughter will be very grateful to get away from boring affairs of state. Where are your plans for sight-seeing?"

Wade sensed the duchess tense beside him and couldn't bring himself betray her. Somehow, somewhere, under that royal facade had to be the woman in white with the sensuous smile he'd been attracted to. A real woman he could reason with. It was up to him to find that woman without making a public deal of it. "Her Grace and I are going to make our plans in the morning."

He heard her sigh of relief. Behind that cool royal exterior and imperious manner there beat the heart of a young woman. A woman who valued her father's approval, even if she didn't value his.

Wade turned to the duchess. "I'll be here to pick you up at nine, Your Grace. But I would appreciate your walking me to the door. With your permission, sir?"

"Of course," the prince remarked. "Go ahead, my dear. I'll be here waiting to say good-night when you return."

May took the arm Wade held out to her as they threaded their way through the thinning crowd. "Thank you for not telling my father we are not in agreement," she said in an undertone. "I am sure I will have a wonderful time in your city. And by the way, you may call me May when we are out in public. It's the name my family calls me. That way no one will know who I really am."

Wade took his cap from an attendant. It was becoming difficult to keep up with the lady's many mood changes, but duty was duty. After a quick glance at the door, he led her back to a quiet corner. "I have two things to say to you before I leave, *May*." He waited until he had her undivided attention.

"One—never, ever stand by a door or a window while you're here in Washington. And maybe not even when you go home. You make too good a target.''

Uneasy at the warning, May glanced around the crowded room. The marine band continued to play, flutes of champagne were still being passed around, and the remaining guests appeared in no hurry to leave. If there were danger here, there was no evidence of it that she could see. ''I'm sure you're exaggerating, Commander. And the second?''

''I'll look over your list, but I have no intention of changing my mind about being the one to decide where we go tomorrow.'' Wade's gaze locked with hers. ''And remember, the Secret Service stays. In the meantime,'' he added softly, ''why don't you put yourself in my hands, Your Grace? I promise you'll enjoy yourself.''

She stared at him, and for a moment her expression softened. For a moment he thought she was going to agree with him. Instead she caught her breath, turned on her heel and headed back to the ballroom.

After being invited to call her May, he could have sworn his charge was about to turn into a human being instead of an imperious royal. Maybe it was just as well she'd walked away when she had. If she hadn't, he would have been tempted to forget the lady had a motive of her own. Or to forget how much he'd been attracted to her.

Futile dreams, he told himself with a sigh of regret as he left for his apartment. He and the duchess were two strangers passing in the night. She'd been born to the cushioned life of a member of a royal family where her every wish was a command. He was a former All-America basketball hero turned lawyer who'd worked for everything he had. By her standards that couldn't be much.

He'd have to play out the next few days carefully. He had to stop thinking about his never-to-be-realized attraction to the beautiful and sensuous lady in white and the invitation in her eyes.

He had to concentrate on not only protecting the duchess from herself; he had to protect her from him.

TO EASE WADE'S WORRY about security, his access to the Blair House the next morning was screened by the same two Secret Service men he'd noticed the evening before.

"No uniform today, Commander?" The older of the two identified himself as Samuel Hoskins and his partner as Mike Wheeler.

"No," Wade replied with a tight smile, replacing his identification in the inside pocket of his loose-fitting jacket. "I was hoping to fade into the landscape."

"With a charge like the duchess, good luck,"

Hoskins murmured as he eyed the gun and holster Wade wore under his jacket. "I see you're prepared."

"Yeah," Wade answered as he shifted shoulders unaccustomed to the weight of the gun and holster. "Is the duchess up and ready?"

"She's finishing breakfast. Said to tell you she'd overslept but would be out in a minute."

Wade nodded. He hadn't slept much last night. Instead he'd spent the hours lying awake thinking about the intriguing duchess and the amusing way she'd tried to assert her independence. In some ways, in her imperious way of speaking and in her assertive manner, she was an echo of the past. But the chances she was late because she'd lain awake thinking of him was wishful thinking. Royalty and the common man were like oil and water—they didn't mix. And neither did he and the duchess.

As for the Secret Service, the duchess had been right. In their navy-blue suits, white shirts and black ties, they were a little on the conservative side; however, they did fade into the landscape. Only the small official button in their coat lapels gave them away.

The duchess didn't know it yet, but at thirty-six, he was just as conservative as they were. At least when he was on duty. It wasn't only the duchess's life that could be at stake. It was his future, too.

And, like everything he took on, he intended to take this tour of duty seriously.

He eyed his two navy-clad partners. "How about you guys? Ready to roll?"

"We'll be right on your tail," Agent Wheeler assured him. "But it would help to know where you're going."

Wade shrugged his shoulders. "First stop is Wal-Mart. After that, who knows? You'll have to wait until I get a chance to talk to the duchess."

Their eyes swung to the lady in question when she finally sailed into the room. To Wade's dismay, she was dressed in her version of dressing down—white linen slacks and matching fitted jacket and a green silk shirt that almost matched the color of her eyes. Green pumps were on her feet and a large straw bag hung from one shoulder. He was relieved to see she wasn't wearing any valuable jewelry he had to worry about.

"No uniform today?" She looked disappointed.

"Not today," he replied. If she'd asked for him as an escort solely because of his uniform, she was out of luck. "Today we're going to play at being ordinary folk."

Ordinary folk. Wade smothered a remark when she raised her eyebrows. No way was the lady going to be able to play at being ordinary. Not when she looked as if she'd just stepped off the cover of *Elle* magazine.

"Wal-Mart, here we come," he muttered under his breath. "Is there someplace private where we can talk before we leave?"

She handed him a slip of paper. "If this is what you wish to talk about, I've already made a list of the places I want to see."

Wade glanced at the list. Planet Hollywood. Hard Rock Café. The antique shops at the Capitol Hill District. The infamous grunge Morgan-Hill shopping area. The list went on and included places Wade knew from experience were definitely not for royal visitors. Especially one who could be the target of troublemakers.

The only item on the list he felt comfortable with was the National Portrait Gallery. He sighed and pocketed the slip of paper.

"We can decide later," he said with a sidelong glance at the fashionable royal outfit. "First, we have to buy you some less obtrusive clothing."

Over the duchess's protests, he stopped to tell the Secret Service men to follow him before he hailed a cab. No way was he going to travel around D.C. in a black unmarked car that broadcast Secret Service presence.

"No car?" Her eyebrows rose suspiciously.

"Not today. It's in for repairs." He handed her

into the cab and directed the driver to Wal-Mart. The duchess looked annoyed when she walked in the door, but thank goodness she kept her thoughts to herself. If she didn't know what Wal-Mart was, she was in for a surprise. "Anyway, Your Grace, after we get through shopping, we'll probably get by more easily by taking the tourmobile around the mall."

"Tourmobile? Mall?" The Duchess frowned. "They are not on my list."

"Maybe not," Wade replied. "But they are on mine."

He had to give the duchess credit when she bit her bottom lip and silently browsed her way through racks of inexpensive brightly colored summer clothing.

May refused to let her temper show. She'd agreed to dress down but she wasn't thrilled about the variety of choices. Designer clothing was more what she was accustomed to wearing. Still, an agreement was an agreement if it would get her to where she wanted to go.

She had put the National Portrait Gallery and a few well-known museums on her list to throw her escort off the track. The Capitol Hill District and its antique shops were surely someplace where she was sure she could lose herself, or maybe even the Morgan-Hill grunge shops. No matter how her escort might protest, she told herself, she intended to draw the line at stone monuments.

She had had it with men controlling her life. If the commander persisted in trying to control her, she would make his job very difficult. For these few days at least, it would be just a matter of time before she would be on her own and have a chance to be true to herself.

She hid her satisfaction as she browsed through the hanging racks. One by one she handed Wade a pair of size-six blue-denim slacks and an oversize sweatshirt with a U.S. flag and Washington, D.C., written across the front in large red, white and blue letters. When he silently pointed to her shoes, she bit her lower lip and headed for the shoe department to try on a pair of sturdy white athletic shoes.

"Anything else?"

Wade bit back a comment and motioned for her to wait while he checked out the dressing room. When he indicated the coast was clear, she sniffed and headed inside to change. But not before she threw him a look that conveyed her opinion of him. It wasn't good.

With the duchess safely behind a closed door, Wade checked to make sure the Secret Service men were still in the vicinity. When he finally located the two in the sports department, he snorted his disgust.

It was beginning to look as if the care and feeding of the duchess was largely going to be up to him.

Twenty minutes later the duchess finally emerged from the dressing room in her new clothing. To his relief, she wasn't the duchess Mary Louise any longer. She was the woman he'd asked her to be. And a damn cute one at that.

"Is this dressed down enough for you?"

Lost in admiration, Wade silently nodded. With her chestnut hair curling loosely around her shoulders, she looked like a typical tourist, courtesy Wal-Mart. He knew, as sure as he knew his own name, as he checked her over, that even as May she would never be able to fade into the landscape.

Gowned in white chiffon or dressed in jeans and a garish sweatshirt no duchess would willingly wear, she was the most beautiful and desirable woman he'd ever met. For a moment he was taken aback. Then he reminded himself he was here as the duchess's temporary escort and that his reactions were out of order.

He shrugged and, for a brief few moments, felt guilty. He watched her looking into a full-length mirror. Most women would have chewed him out by now for being so controlling. To add to his misgivings, behind the jeans and colorful sweatshirt there was something about the look in her eyes that told him she wasn't as docile as she appeared to be. She would bear watching.

The Secret Service agents, back from checking out fishing rods, silently looked at each other.

Wade put the clothing the duchess had worn into the store into a shopping cart and headed for the checkout counters. The duchess, with the Secret Service trailing behind her, followed.

He might have been a success in creating the all-American girl next door, Wade thought in despair. But, heaven help him, the lady looked just as royal and just as unattainable as she'd been before.

Chapter Three

"*This* is the mall?" May clutched the only item from her original clothing choice Wade had allowed her to keep, her large straw bag. The rest of her possessions were locked in the trunk of the unmarked black sedan driven by the Secret Service and, to her disgust, was safely out of her reach. "I thought you meant a shopping mall!"

As if she'd said something amusing, Wade burst out laughing. "No, Your Grace, what you see is a lot more than that." He motioned to the series of buildings in front of them. "Those are only a few of the Smithsonian museums. There are nine of them."

"Museums," May echoed faintly. She was tempted to tell him she'd visited dozens of museums and churches as part of her duties back home and wasn't looking forward to spending time seeing any more. She shuddered. "You can't possibly mean we're going to visit all nine, do you?"

"No," he looked at his watch. "We don't have time. But maybe tomorrow. Today you can take your pick of the National Museum of American History, the Museum of Natural History, the National Gallery of Art or the Arts and Industry Museum—"

"Stop right there," she commanded, peering at her escort. "You *are* joking, are you not?"

"Not at all," he replied cheerfully, amused at her quaint manner of speech. "If these don't appeal to you, there are a few more museums farther on that might interest you."

"No, thank you." May had to fight the urge to lose herself in the passing stream of tourists. If only she hadn't outsmarted herself by wearing a garish sweatshirt bound to stand out in any crowd. "What else is on your list?"

Wade made a show of consulting a slip of paper he'd taken out of his jacket pocket. "We can take the trolley to the other end of the Mall and check out the Capitol Building, if you're interested. Or grab a cab and visit the Jefferson Memorial. It's beautiful, especially at dusk. I'm sure you'll like it. In fact, the memorial is my personal favorite."

"Maybe so," May answered, her mind busy trying to find a way to lose her escort. "But dusk is a long way off. On second thought,'' she added, ''how about the National Portrait Gallery? It *is* somewhere around here, is it not?'' With an excuse to use the ladies' room she was sure she would be able to rid herself of the garish sweatshirt that marked her. Once out of her escort's sight, and dressed like the average tourist, surely it would be easy to get lost in a crowd when he wasn't looking.

He looked surprised. ''You really want to visit the National Portrait Gallery?''

''Sure,'' she said, pretending innocence. ''It *was* on my list, wasn't it?''

''Yes, it was,'' Wade agreed, but he didn't look convinced. ''Frankly, I thought you only put it on the list to throw me off.''

''You don't trust me?'' She widened her eyes and tried to look innocent.

''Ask me no questions…'' His voice trailed off.

May winced as she remembered the universally well-known finish of the saying: …and I'll tell you no lies.

She managed to look wounded, her mind made up. What had put Wade on to her, anyway? She had told the truth. Even if there was an ulterior motive behind it.

''Let us go,'' she said with a tight smile. ''According to you, my life could be in danger, so do not forget to call me May in public.''

Wade smothered a reply. Her facetious response told him she wasn't aware of any possible danger to her or she wouldn't be taking things so casually. How could he protect her when she didn't think she needed to be protected? And especially when she was obviously bent on having her way, one way or another?

He silently cursed the undersecretary of the navy for involving him in the current scenario. And with a secret that should never have been kept from the person at risk. Without her cooperation, his assignment was much riskier.

All the more reason to protect the lady from herself.

"Let's go." He took her arm but not before glancing behind him for the two Secret Service agents who should have been there but were not.

It looked as if, for now at least, he and the duchess were on their own.

He picked up a couple of brochures on the way into the gallery and handed one to the duchess. "Everything around you is a portrait or possession of an American who contributed in some way to our country." He pointed out well-known portraits and memorabilia in glass cases that dated back to the eighteenth century. "Take your pick."

She studied the brochure he handed her and moved down the room. He had to give her credit for being a good sport, but after about forty portraits he noticed her attention was flagging. ''Want a break?'' he asked sympathetically.

''I could use a chance to freshen up,'' she said as they passed the door to a ladies' room. Before he could reply, she disappeared behind the mahogany door.

After making sure there was only one way in and out of the rest room, Wade lounged alongside the door. While something told him she had something up her sleeve, surely a stop at the ladies' room was no big deal.

But what *was* a big deal was that he had an uneasy feeling they'd been followed. He gazed at his surroundings. Crowds of people, families with children and, from the sound of conversation, a number of foreign visitors. So far, so good.

He finally spotted the two Secret Service agents covertly studying a burly, dark-haired man down the hall. Maybe it was the sight of the man that made the hackles rise on the back of his neck, but there was something definitely going on. He was debating moving away from the rest room door to confront the man when he disappeared. The Secret Service agents with him.

Uneasy, Wade vowed to be extra watchful from here on out. And not to let the intriguing and conniving duchess, or anyone else, distract him from his duty to protect her.

Heaven help him if he lost a charge for the second time.

After a few minutes he checked his watch. Not even a duchess needed more than twenty minutes to freshen up, he told himself. He'd been right from the moment he'd heard about the escort duty, he thought sourly. What the lady needed was a nursemaid or a nanny. A woman who could charge through that closed door and haul her out of there, willing or not.

A woman with two little girls about to enter the ladies' room paused to glance suspiciously at him. He straightened up and sighed. Much more of this and he would be arrested for loitering outside a women's rest room.

"Pardon me, ma'am," he said hurriedly. "I wonder if you could do me a favor. My girlfriend's inside. She's been in there so long I'm beginning to worry about her. Do you mind asking if there's a May inside? And reminding her, her boyfriend is out here waiting for her?"

The woman's frown disappeared and was replaced by a sympathetic smile. "Not at all, young man. I'll send her right out."

A moment later Wade saw May sneak out and turn left—the wrong direction for the exit.

Eyes popping, Wade almost didn't recognize her. She wore a too-tight T-shirt she must have hidden under the large Wal-Mart sweatshirt. He edged after her, keeping a hulking father of five between the two of them.

He was surprised to see her pause. Her profile, her downturned mouth caught his attention. What could she have been looking at? He edged closer and peered over a tourist's shoulder. To his surprise, she was looking at a family portrait that included two children, one of them a baby.

Before he could speak up, the duchess turned around and made for the exit.

His fears realized, Wade gritted his teeth. Whatever the duchess thought she was doing, she was no match for him. In three quick strides he caught her by her arm. "You're not going to get rid of me that easily, Your Grace, or should I say May?"

She glanced at his hand. She looked surprised but, thank God, didn't lose her cool. He smothered a sigh of relief and took his hand away. Maybe he ought to remember whom he was dealing with. A duchess was a duchess, after all.

"May," she said. Her voice soft, the look in her eyes inviting. But he knew the truth. She was putting on an act.

She might have invited him to call her by her nickname, but from her first reaction to his holding her arm, Wade doubted anyone of the lady's acquaintance, outside of her immediate family, had ever been so familiar with her. So why was she allowing him to touch her?

"May it is," he agreed, "but don't bother to tempt me." He eyed her formfitting T-shirt, her lush lips and intriguing eyes. To his disgust his body stirred. No matter how she was dressed, the lady was trouble in the form of an inviting bundle of femininity. If he knew what was good for him, he'd keep his testosterone under control and remember he was just her bodyguard.

Out of the corner of his eye, he spotted the helpful woman and her two little girls coming out of the ladies' room and heading toward them. He put his arms around the duchess and mentally prayed she was smart enough to go along with him.

"Pardon me, ma'am," he said. "My girlfriend forgot her sweatshirt back inside there. It's the one with Washington, D.C., written across the front in large red, white and blue letters. You can't miss it. Do you mind bringing it out for her? I'm afraid she's cold without it."

The woman was frankly curious and eyed May. "Why can't she go inside and get it for herself?"

He gripped the duchess even tighter and felt her strain against him. "I'm afraid she'll get lost inside there again. We have an important appointment to keep.''

The woman nodded reluctantly, went back inside the rest room and came out with the sweatshirt. With a reproving glance at the duchess, she led the children away.

''A leash,'' Wade echoed softly, glancing down at the woman he held in his arms. ''Not a bad idea, considering. Now, stay still for a moment.'' He turned the duchess around to face him. ''Are you going to come quietly or...'' He slipped the bulky sweatshirt over her head while he spoke. Big mistake. He'd not only seen the duchess's very feminine curves under the T-shirt, his hands were sliding over her warm torso. Just how much was a red-blooded man expected to take, he asked himself as he pulled the sweatshirt into place and stepped back. ''Now you look like a real tourist again.''

She glanced down at the shirt and shrugged. ''If you say so. Now what, Commander?''

''We could we go back to the galleries, or maybe you're ready for something else?''

''Lunch would be nice,'' she answered with a startled look. ''Unless you intend to starve me into submission.''

''Not at all,'' he said as he sensed she had been just as affected by his hands sliding over her as he had been. And that she had to be aware of his body's involuntary response at the contact. Not that he could have helped responding to her warm skin, lush curves and silky smile. He would have had to be carved out of marble not to react. "I'm a twenty-first-century man. Torture isn't my style. Where would you like to eat?"

"I'm a stranger here, remember?" She gazed around the gallery. "This visit has been very educational, but I'd like to go someplace where there's the sound of human voices, perhaps some music. I don't mean to offend you, Commander," she added as if in apology, "but I'd like to go somewhere more exciting."

"Call me Wade," he said, glancing at the portraits of men and women who made him proud to serve his country. She was right. Maybe, to a casual foreign observer, the gallery wasn't as exciting as it was to him.

Still, the feeling they were being watched was exciting enough for him. Maybe it *was* better to move on. "Let's go. I know just the place."

Outside, the elusive Secret Service men were nowhere to be seen. Wade hailed a cab and opened the door for his companion. Thank goodness, she was back to smiling. And this time, he sensed the smile was genuine. "The Old Post Office Pavilion, driver."

"Oh, no," May said unhappily as she scooted

across the seat to make room for him. "Not a post office!"

"Take my word for it, *May*," he said with a warning glance at the cab driver, "this isn't like any post office you've ever seen. You're going to like this one."

She did. Fascinated by the renovated nineteenth-century Romanesque building, May gazed happily around her at the laughing crowds milling around. And at the double level of shops selling food and items from around the world. She had told the truth, she was starving.

To her delight a band was playing at one end of the first floor. A female singer was belting out "Hit or Miss," a song she vaguely recognized was a popular American love song. And, as a result of the beautiful melody, reacted even more strongly than ever to her male escort's presence at her side.

She silently chided herself for her futile attraction to Wade Stevens. An attraction she had felt when she had first noticed him. An attraction that would linger long after she was back home.

She returned her attention to her surroundings with an effort. Her escort had delivered, just as he'd promised. The old post office was a taste of the excitement and a part of the city she'd been hoping to experience.

"What would you like to eat?"

"Something typically American," she answered. "My father brought his chef with him, and the food is the same as we have back home."

"You'll find American food here," he told her as he pointed to the food stalls. "What will it be, May? Name it and I'm sure it's probably available."

"Mexican," she answered happily, eyeing a neon sign. "It looks and smells inviting. But are you sure it's typically American?"

"It is now," Wade said as he spied a table being vacated in front of the fast-food stall. "You grab a table and I'll get the food." The temptation to find a vacant table momentarily threatened to overwhelm his common sense.

"Oh, no," she said, pulling back. "I want to look at everything. And order a little of everything that looks good. You take the table. I'll be right back."

Wade caught her arm. After her extended stay in the ladies' room, he wasn't about to let her go off on her own. Not while he still had his marbles. He intended to spend the rest of the day joined at the hip to the duchess. "The answer is no. We'll go together," he said firmly, and took her arm. "Lead on."

May dug in her heels. "You still do not trust me, do you? Where do you think I would go?"

"No farther than I can throw a stick," he said frankly. "The rules are that you're not going anywhere without me. But don't let that spoil your appetite.'' He led her to the Happy Burrito food stall.

To his amusement May was as good as her word. She was either actually starving or she was putting on a good show. She finally headed for a vacant table carrying a tray laden with a variety of Mexican foods. He passed up his turn to order and strode after her. Whatever she'd chosen would have to be enough for two.

Maybe he had been wrong about her, Wade thought as he followed her swaying hips to a newly vacant table. After an amused glance at her full tray, he'd known he wouldn't have to worry about her pulling a disappearing act, at least for a while. She'd be too busy eating.

He sat back and surveyed the territory. They were surrounded by enough people to make up a small army. Foreign visitors mingled with American tourists. Maybe even some visitors from countries surrounding Baronovia, he thought unhappily as he checked out the area. Maybe even some from countries that were apparently determined to block a United States presence there.

He remained troubled as the duchess ate her way through her lunch. She glanced up as she dug a corn chip into small plastic dish of hot salsa and held it up to his lips. ''Would you like to share?''

Mesmerized by the way she licked a bit of salsa

from her lips, Wade opened his mouth for the spicy tidbit. When her fingers grazed his lips, his heart skipped a beat or two. As long as this was a game, he was a willing participant. But that was as far as he intended to go. "Kind of spicy, isn't it?"

She dipped another corn chip into salsa and chewed happily. Another bit of salsa clung to the corner of her lips. Instinctively he leaned forward and wiped it away with a gentle fingertip. Their eyes met. Hers were wide with a question.

He didn't know what she was thinking, but he realized his gesture had been more intimate than it should have been. Damn! Much more of this and he'd be putty in her hands. "Just trying to be helpful," he said.

"Thank you," she said with a winsome smile. "I find I like Mexican food. I shall have to find a way to bring it to Baronovia."

Wade thought rapidly. No matter if she'd invited him to call her May while in public, even in private, touching her was not appropriate behavior for an escort. Why had the duchess welcomed his intimate touch? Was it an act?

Or, more to the point, was she now the real May and no longer the devious duchess Mary Louise?

As if to remind him he was her bodyguard as well as her escort, the holster and his Beretta dug into the side of his chest. At the reminder, he tensed and casually glanced around to make sure no one was paying undue attention to them. He would have felt a lot better about being so exposed to danger if he could be certain the Secret Service had caught up with them.

Her appetite momentarily satisfied, May gazed happily around her. The Old Post Office and the air of excitement generated by the hundreds of tourists were just what she wanted to experience. Stone tributes honoring the American heroes she'd known from studying history books were not.

She understood her escort's appreciation of the places she had said she wanted to visit. The commander was, in or out of the uniform that had attracted her, in the service of his country.

She would have been pleased if he'd worn his uniform now.

She shouldn't complain, she thought as she gazed at Wade Stevens. Dressed in beige slacks, loose matching jacket and a white shirt open to his throat, he looked like an ordinary tourist. What he couldn't hide was that he was a military man. At least, not to her. She'd reviewed enough military parades in the company of her father to recognize the proud demeanor and the assurance of a military man.

She yearned to be plain May Baron. To have a man like Wade for her own. To have the child she hadn't been able to conceive when she was married.

Foolish dreams, she told herself and lowered her eyes. She was a dowager duchess with a future royal role yet to be played.

"That was very delicious, thank you," she said as she wiped her lips. "Dessert?"

Wade eyed her middle that was covered with the garish sweatshirt and visualized the supple form hidden underneath. "You can't possibly have room in there for another bite!"

"I don't want to miss anything," she protested. "Besides, I was only thinking about a chocolate sundae, nothing too big."

Nothing big turned out to be a sundae, dripping with chocolate syrup and covered with tiny bits of nuts.

"Keep that up and your clothes aren't going to fit," Wade murmured.

May was aware she should have been offended at her escort's familiarity, but she actually enjoyed his friendly banter. To her pleasure he was behaving as if she were actually May and he her boyfriend or husband. She smiled impishly at him. "Don't worry, the sweatshirt will hide it all."

Not in a million years, Wade thought—just as he knew he'd never forget how her body felt when he'd slid the sweatshirt over her shoulders. Soft, warm and made to fit a man's hands. His.

He shrugged off his sensuous thoughts as they

strolled around the shops and tried to ignore the inviting ice cream and chocolate scent of his companion.

Just like a typical tourist, the duchess chose a few souvenirs, including a tiny replica of the Statue of Liberty. "Where to now?"

She gazed at him expectantly. "You mean I get to choose?"

"Yes, as long as I approve of your choice."

Her pleasure melted as quickly as the sundae melted in its plastic cup. She'd wanted to be an ordinary tourist during her stay in Washington, had even invited Wade to treat her as May. But enough was enough. If he'd known her better, he would have understood he had not only crossed the invisible line between them, he would have known he reminded her of her controlling late husband. She lost her interest in the sundae and tossed the cup into a receptacle. "*You* approve? I don't think so. Only my father has the right to dictate to me," she said ominously.

"Look here, May," he said in a firm undertone. "We've been through this before. I thought you understood I'm more than your escort. I'm also your bodyguard."

Her eyes narrowed. "Nonsense. I am the Dowager Duchess of Lorrania. Who would want to harm me?"

Wade debated sharing the information Undersecretary Logan had told him. He might have agreed to keep all the facts private, but he somehow had to get his charge off her high horse, if only for her own good. The only way she was sure to cooperate with him without an argument would be to reveal as much of the truth as he could without giving away the whole story. He'd deal with Logan if and when the time came.

"Come with me," he said, his mind made up. Proper protocol or not he was the man assigned to keep her out of danger, and no amount of protocol was going to get in his way.

He took the duchess by the arm and led her to a quiet corner of the building. "I don't know if your father told you all the reasons for your state visit, Your Grace, but I'm going to share some of them with you. First of all, I believe I should explain why the State Department is so interested in your welfare. That is, if you're willing to hear me out and promise not to become ballistic over what you hear."

She frowned. "Ballistic?"

"Right," he answered. "I can handle anything but a hysterical woman."

"Then you don't know me very well," she said proudly. "I never become hysterical. Life as a member of Baronovia's royal family has not always been a bed of roses. Besides, even roses have thorns. What do you have to tell me?''

Wade mentally prayed for guidance. ''You are aware that my country is hoping to turn our trade mission in Baronovia into an embassy?''

She frowned. ''Yes, of course. Surely that is not the problem?''

He couldn't tell her the details of the State Department's secret plans for the embassy, but damn it, maybe he could tell her just enough to get her attention. ''No, Your Grace. The problem is that some of the countries surrounding Baronovia aren't too happy about your visit here.''

''And what precisely can they do about it?'' she asked, back to being every inch the royal. ''Baronovia is a sovereign nation and is recognized by the United Nations as a neutral country.''

He took a deep breath. He was in too deep but couldn't go the whole nine yards. Nor could he risk getting in over his head.

''There have been rumors of discontent in the countries surrounding Baronovia,'' he went on. ''I also hear that protests are being lodged with our State Department even as we speak. Bottom line, Your Grace,'' he said with all the sincerity he could muster, ''the State Department and the prince, your father, all believe you could be in danger.''

A look of doubt passed over her face. Disbelief

shadowed her eyes. "My father? Why hasn't he told me of this?"

"I'm sure he didn't want to worry you."

"And is that why your people were so obliging when I requested you for my escort?" she asked. Her eyes grew cool. "Because you are part of the military and it is your duty to obey?"

"Yes." May obviously wasn't happy. The truth was that once he knew her, he would have volunteered to guard her. He decided to hedge. "They were aware I've had some training as a bodyguard."

"And when you've behaved as if you were interested in me, it was an act? You were only doing your duty?"

Wade forced himself to nod his agreement. But not before he found himself wishing he could tell her his interest in her wasn't all from duty. He didn't understand why, but he was beginning to care for her in ways that turned his senses on fire.

Since his duties with JAG called for him to travel the world at a moment's notice, romance had always taken a back seat. Until he'd been assigned to guard May. The bodyguard assignment might have started out as an undesirable duty, but the truth was he'd been hooked the moment he'd thought of her as his lady in white. Now, he had to keep his distance from her because the only way he could protect her was to stay uninvolved.

A sadness came over her eyes again. He could tell she felt betrayed by her father and maybe, even, by him. Duty be damned when it hurt the woman he was beginning to care for. But he couldn't tell her the truth.

"I'm sorry, Your Grace," he said gently. "I didn't mean to upset you. But since it's my duty to protect you, I felt you should know some of the facts in the case. So, if there's nothing else you'd like to see today, I'll take you back to the Blair House."

"No. I wish to continue our tour." May lifted her head proudly. She was a duchess and not to be cowed by vague threats. Nor by an overly officious attractive military man who pretended to care for her for duty's sake. No matter what the eventual truth of their relationship turned out to be, she wasn't the kind of woman to cower under her bed. "I still wish to visit the Hard Rock Café and Planet Hollywood. Shall we go?"

She waved her hand, a gesture Wade knew all to well by now: his concerns were being dismissed. Her facial expression was calm, but her eyes gave her away. She was hurt.

"Yes, Your Grace," Wade said quietly. "We'll go, but back to the Blair House. I'm not comfortable without Secret Service backup. I'm sure your father and the State Department would agree if they knew."

She threw him a cool look he would remember for a long time.

Strangely enough, rather than resenting the duchess's imperious attitude, he found himself wondering what might have been between them if this had been another time and another place. If they hadn't come from two different worlds.

To his chagrin what troubled him the most was how he could remain so suspicious of the duchess, and at the same time be so attracted to her.

Chapter Four

Wade was hard put not to give away his dark thoughts as he studied the new list the duchess handed him the next morning. From the way things were adding up, it looked as if the lady wasn't going to be any easier to deal with today than she had been yesterday.

Good thing they were in the foyer of the Blair House where he still had some control of the situation. And from the look in her eyes, it was some, not much.

Royalty or not, intrigued by her or not, the beautiful Dowager Duchess Mary Louise of Baronovia was on the verge of becoming a pain in the neck. He had to remind himself that the lady was a VIP visitor to his country and that his future depended on keeping her safe.

"As I told you yesterday, Your Grace," he said in as reasonable tone he could muster, "believe me, some of the places you've listed here aren't safe to visit. Are you sure you want to go there?"

"Yes, I am. Besides," she said with an elusive smile he knew damn well was intended to flatter hi, "you are an officer in the United States Navy, are you not? With your background, and if you were to wear your uniform, I'm sure you will be able to handle any small problem that might come along."

Wade shook his head. Underneath that studied smile of the duchess was a woman of fire, a woman willing to seduce him with a look to get her way. It wasn't working. No matter how thick she piled it on, he wasn't buying. He was on to her, and as intelligent as she appeared to be, surely she had to know it.

"Uniforms are a dime a dozen in D.C., Your Grace," he said with a smile. "Mine doesn't impress anyone. Besides, I'm not going to be in uniform. We're trying to look like normal tourists, remember?"

She looked disappointed and gazed woefully down at her sweatshirt.

Wade bit back a smile at the look of distaste that came over her face. Considering the way she'd looked in her glamorous white chiffon dress when he'd first noticed her at the Baronovia cocktail party, she had his sympathy. The situation would have been comical if the need to have his charge look like a normal tourist weren't so serious.

He surveyed the large red, white and blue letters on her shirt that spelled out Washington, D.C. As if they weren't loud enough to attract attention, the addition of the red, white and blue American flag seemed to flutter when she took a deep breath. He didn't like the sweatshirt any more than the duchess did but it was a hell of a cover.

Of course, he mused, the disguise worked only if a man didn't notice her sparkling, exotic green eyes or the dimples that danced across her cheeks when she smiled. Or if a man were able to ignore the tantalizing spicy scent that lingered around her.

He sighed at the futility of it all. No matter how she was dressed, the lady was bound to draw second glances. Coupled with the graceful way she carried herself, the duchess made an impressive feminine package that was a dead giveaway. There was nothing ordinary about her. Not that what he thought about how she was dressed made a difference. He was her bodyguard. And he'd do whatever it took to keep her safe and out of harm's way.

He smothered his runaway thoughts and glanced at the new list one more time. "The Capitol Hill District? What's the matter, doesn't Baronovia have enough art and antique shops for you?"

"Of course, but not Americana," she said wistfully as she gazed at the graceful Thomas Jefferson cherry wood desk with a glass top that sat in the center of the library. "You may not believe me, Commander, but I am very impressed with your country, and not only with the food. I have my heart set on bringing home a few items to remind me of my visit."

He thought of the odds and ends back home on the family farm in Nebraska. Items the duchess would probably consider Americana and want to own if only he could show them to her. He would have liked to show her farm life, too, if she were actually telling the truth and not putting him on.

After second thoughts Wade nodded. If the duchess were really taken with the United States, visiting the Capitol Hill District and its collection of antiques and American art sounded like a reasonable request. Now if only he could get the shopping trip out of the way without any problems.

One thought led to another.

He'd been kept too busy to think of home and his family in recent months. Even though he'd chosen the navy for his career seventeen years ago, Nebraska and the family farm remained a part of him.

As he gazed at the wistful look in the duchess's eyes, he began to wish there were some way to show her the rural America he loved. Washington, D.C., was awesome in its own way, but the sweeping wheat fields, blue skies and Nebraska air, so clean it actually smelled sweet, was awesome, too. There people looked you in the eye when they said, "How are you," and meant it when they said they were glad to see you.

He wondered what childhood memories the duchess carried with her. Were they happy? Satisfying? Judging from the little he knew about the way royalty lived, he had his doubts.

He checked her list again. This time, instead of dismissing it out of hand, he decided there had to be something he could show his charge that would please her. He read on.

The next item was a rock concert scheduled to be held in Rock Creek Park, a benefit for the hungry children of the world. But exposing her to that kind of milieu was definitely not a good idea.

"A rock concert?" he asked, horrified at the possibility of keeping hundreds of rock music enthusiasts from trampling his charge. "You've got to be kidding!"

"Why? I thought all Americans like rock concerts. Besides I understand it is for a very worthy cause." She looked genuinely puzzled.

"Not this American," he said, shivering at the memory of the few outdoor rock concerts he'd attended.

This time she looked shocked. "You don't like music?"

Maybe it was an ego trip, but somehow Wade didn't want to lose the little esteem the duchess might have for him. Somehow, for reasons he wasn't too clear about yet, he was beginning to care about her opinion of him.

He had to talk fast to distract her, he told himself as he studied the list again. The more rowdy places were out, no matter what she said. As for the Capitol Hill District, it was growing more attractive by the minute. Shopping for antiques or artwork had to be a hell of a lot better than the uncertainty of a rock concert—benefit or not.

"Sure, I do," he answered. "I actually play a mean guitar. As for liking music—rock music, yes. Rock concerts, no. A person can get himself killed out there."

Her eyes lit up. "You play a guitar? For your own amusement?"

He'd diverted her from rock concerts, all right, but now that the subject was himself it was becoming difficult to keep their relationship formal.

He smiled wryly. "Sure. I had my own band while I was growing up. But looking back at our lack of success, I'd say you're probably right. I was playing for my own amusement."

She appeared pleased as he confessed a secret he

usually kept to himself. To add to his misery, confessing that he'd failed at a project he'd taken on was nothing to be proud of. Except that she actually looked interested. He hurried on before he found himself baring his soul. "That was then, this is now. Benefit concert or not, rock concerts are definitely out."

Her smile faded. "You're becoming paranoid, Commander. I'm beginning to think you see danger everywhere, even when there is none. Music is music—all kinds. As for keeping me away from a rock concert, I told you before that I refuse to live in a cage, gilded or not."

He smothered another sigh and checked the list again. His spirits picked up when a thought hit him. "If it's music you want, I hear there's a concert in the park tomorrow night."

To Wade's relief, instead of behaving like the royal she actually was, and more like the girl next door she was pretending to be, the duchess made a face. Maybe there actually *was* a real woman hidden under the royal persona.

He accepted the inevitable. He would meet the duchess halfway. Anyone who truly admired Washington deserved to see as much of the city as he in good conscience could show her.

"Tell you what," he conceded as he motioned behind him and started toward the front door. "I've decided we can go over to the Capitol Hill District, after all. You can browse and shop and get it out of your system. When you've had enough, I'll find a typically American restaurant for lunch. And as a special treat," he added, "I'll show you my favorite spot in D.C.—the Jefferson Memorial at dusk. How about it?"

She nodded enthusiastically. "I would like that. That way there will be a little something for you as well as something for me."

"It's all for you, Your Grace," he said, warming to her wide smile. As far as he was concerned, it was the first genuine smile she'd shown him since he'd been asked to become her bodyguard. And maybe it was a glimpse of the real woman without pretenses. "I've been there and done that."

Her eyebrows rose. Too late, he realized she probably wondered just what he meant by "been there and done that." Considering some of things he'd managed to get himself into before he reached the age of reason, he hoped she would think of him as an upstanding officer in the United States Navy.

"Before we go, Your Grace, we need to set some ground rules."

She grimaced. "More rules? I thought I had heard them all by now. I also thought I was supposed to enjoy myself during this visit to your city."

"Maybe so, but the rules bear repeating—or I'm

afraid you might not enjoy yourself." He eyed the rebellion growing in her eyes warily. How was he supposed to say no to a duchess, anyway?

To his relief she nodded. May was like a chameleon, her body language changing by the moment. One moment she was a seductive siren, the next an eager shopper and in between an imperious royal.

Behind him he heard a Secret Service agent cough. Reminded of his proper place in her life, and uneasy at the way his charge was beginning to affect him, Wade forged ahead.

"Number one, while we're out there, you're May and I'm Wade."

"No problem," she shrugged. "Next?"

"Number two, you go where I go and do what I tell you to do."

Her lips tightened. He took a deep breath. Now came the really hard part.

"Number three, the Secret Service escort goes along with us."

"Agreed," she said after a moment's pause, but he could tell she wasn't pleased. "Now, shall we go?"

Wade stuffed the list into his pocket and thrust the image of May as the girl next door away from his mind, the mental trip to his family farm included. This was strictly a business assignment, he reminded himself. He should have remembered he was a sucker for exotic green eyes and dimpled cheeks. And for her spicy scent that reminded him of one of his more glamorous assignments that had taken him to orange groves on Mediterranean shores. And where gentle night breezes drifted over warm waters. Much more of his mental wanderings and he was afraid he'd wind up putty in her hands.

After covertly checking to see his Beretta was firmly in place, he gave her a pointed look and led the way to the front door. But not before checking to make sure the Secret Service agents unpeeled themselves from the walls and were following them.

To his horror, when he opened the front door of the Blair House he found himself with something more to worry about than planning a quiet sightseeing afternoon.

In the short time since he'd arrived at the Blair House, a protest group had shown up.

A few protesters were dressed in their native dress. Some were carrying Baronovia national flags. Others were waving signs that said, Keep Baronovia a Free Country, Keep Baronovia Neutral and No United States Embassy in Baronovia. Off to the side on a corner of Lafayette Park, an impassioned speaker surrounded by curiosity seekers, was shouting in a foreign language and pointing to the Blair

House. At the sight of May in the doorway, a barrage of rotten tomatoes sailed their way.

To Wade's amazement it looked as if the people of Baronovia were actually protesting against their own rulers! And, even more surprising, were against the supposedly proposed ''secret'' alliance between their country and the United States. He swore under his breath, secret mission, was it? Like hell! The news of the proposed alliance was sure to be plastered across every newspaper in the country by morning.

On the other hand, he told himself over the thundering of his heart, the protesters could have been planted by small countries surrounding Baronovia. Countries that opposed any further alliance between the two countries. Either way the protest was rapidly turning into a worst-case scenario: the duchess's safety was at risk. He loosened his jacket and felt for his Beretta.

Agent Mike Wheeler spoke into the cell phone attached to his wrist and stepped in front of the duchess.

Even as Wheeler spoke, a rock sailed past Wade's ear and crashed into the door behind him. Wailing sirens sounded across Pennsylvania Avenue. Two D.C. police helicopters appeared overhead. What had started as a peaceful demonstration was rapidly turning into a potentially violent one.

Wade grabbed his surprised charge around her waist and pulled her back into the Blair House. "Wait here," he commanded over her shocked protests. "Better yet, go inside the library and stay away from the door and windows. In fact, don't even move a muscle until I find out what's going on!"

"They are my countrymen," the duchess cried as she struggled to get away from Wade. "They would never harm me! Let me go!"

"How can you be so sure?" He pulled her against him and stared into her shocked eyes. In that moment Wade realized she'd become more than just a woman he was attracted to. She was a woman in danger, possibly for her very life. As her bodyguard, he felt duty-bound to give his own life to make certain she was safe, if necessary. Thank God, it was largely rotten tomatoes they were throwing.

"This doesn't look like a peaceful protest, Your Grace," he pleaded, and closed the door behind him. "Stay here. You might get hurt."

"They speak my language, and you do not," May said as she struggled in his arms. "If you will kindly step aside, I will go out and speak to my people."

He shook his head, drew her away from the door and to the library. "No, ma'am. I can't let you go out there. While I'm sure it's your father they want to hear from, they may harbor some resentment for you.''

Outside the door, he heard the sound of police car sirens, running feet. A clipped voice shouted instructions through a bullhorn for the protesters to disburse. He shuddered as he heard shouts outside as protestors were being arrested. Inside the Blair House, thank God, a measured defense plan was taking place. Men in plain clothes took up their positions alongside the windows. A voice shouted to keep the prince of Baronovia in his suite upstairs. Another demanded to know where the duchess was being held.

"This is Commander Stevens," Wade shouted. "I have the duchess with me. I'm taking her into the library until this is over!"

MAY FINALLY REALIZED Wade wasn't going to let her go no matter how much she pleaded with him. An uneasy feeling swept through her as it became obvious she was in some kind of danger, after all. Common sense overcame her determination to live her life on her own terms.

Her world outside the Blair House may have turned upside down, she thought as she burrowed closer into Wade's chest, but here in his strong arms she felt safe. She felt the rapid pounding of his heart, muscles tense in the arms that held her close. She inhaled his manly scent and welcomed the words of reassurance he murmured into her ear. The scent of a brave man, she thought as she leaned wearily against his chest. A man prepared to defend her with his life. She should be grateful, instead of acting like a spoiled child.

For that matter, she thought wistfully, as the first-born in the ruling family of Baronovia, she'd never been allowed to be a child. Instead she'd been treated as the future ruler of Baronovia from her early teens. It had only been the recent and happy birth of a much younger half brother that had loosened the reins that bound her.

But not soon enough to have allowed her to marry when and with whom she pleased. She'd married the man chosen for her and had been widowed two short years later.

As a young girl she'd often dreamed of a fairy-tale prince who would come one day to rescue her from the boundaries of her palace. He was to have been a strong and handsome man who would look into her heart and make all her dreams come true. Life was to have become a series of adventures away from royalty and the rules that bound them. He was to have been a man like Wade Stevens.

Instead, according to her father's wishes, she'd married Ivan, Duke of Lorrania, a tiny principality adjoining her country. A marriage that had been planned from the moment of her birth and had ended in his death.

Now, instead of a fairy-tale prince come to rescue her, she had another arranged marriage to look forward to. Thank God, with the birth of her half brother, she would be spared becoming Baronovia's ruler with even more rules to bind her—a life she hadn't sought and didn't want.

"Feeling better?" A gentle hand stroked her hair.

As much as she wanted to remain in his arms, even to have him watch over her, May did her duty as a daughter of the ruling house of Baronovia. She straightened and slipped out of his embrace. "Much better, thank you."

Wade cleared his throat, released her and led her into the library and to an upholstered easy chair. "Good. You can wait here while I see what is going on."

She stretched out a hand to stay him. "Wait, please! My father, Prince Alexis. I must know if he is all right."

"I'll check, Your Grace, but there are Secret Service men assigned to guard him. Don't worry. It's unlikely anyone could have come inside the Blair House without their knowledge." He paused when she covered her lips. "Don't worry, protests happen around here all the time. It'll be over before you know it."

"When will you return?" she asked when the silence inside the library suddenly became more frightening than the threatening noise outside.

Wade spoke into the small cell phone attached to his wrist. All he heard was muffled static.

"I'm not going anywhere," he answered. "I'll be right outside the door." He turned back. "By the way, Your Grace, this is a good example of why I was assigned to be your escort, rather, your bodyguard. And why there are rules you must follow in order to keep you safe."

May smiled wearily as he stepped outside. True to his word he left the door open behind him. He was right. The authorities might have planned for her to have a bodyguard during her stay in Washington, but the selection of Commander Wade Stevens of the United States Navy had been hers. A wise choice for real life, she told herself as she heard his strong, reassuring voice outside the door. If only he could have been the fairy-tale prince she'd dreamed of, as well.

Suddenly giving in to the stress she was under, May curled up in a large upholstered chair. Thoughts of Wade filled her head as her eyes closed.

Wade came back into the library to find May asleep, her head burrowed into the corner of the upholstered chair, a trace of a smile curving her lips. Maybe he was being too hard on her, he thought unhappily, but the rules he was asking her to follow were for her own good. She might not have believed him until now, but the protestors outside the Blair House were proof enough she was at risk.

Awake, the duchess was an imperious royal down to her pink toes. Asleep she was a beautiful and vulnerable young woman. While he stood there gazing down on her, a contented sound escaped her flushed lips. Her smile grew. Whatever she was dreaming about, she was happier than when he'd left her.

He hated to awaken her but the two Secret Service agents in an unmarked black car were waiting at the rear entrance of the Blair House.

To his surprise, he did something he'd never thought to do: he touched the tip of her nose with a gentle fingertip. Having her own countrymen turn against her had to be devastating. "May," he said softly, "if you still want to browse the hill for antiques, I have a car waiting for us."

Her eyes opened slowly. A rosy flush tinged her face as she recognized him and shook away her dream. "Wade? Is my father all right?"

"Everything is under control," he answered. "Your father has called an emergency meeting of his staff and the State Department and sends his regrets. He will speak to you later."

She stretched like the contented kittens his mother

always kept back home. "Thank you, yes. However, I would like to freshen up. You will wait for me?"

"I'll wait right here," Wade assured her. He watched her slim figure in the ridiculous Wal-Mart sweatshirt hurry out the door.

By now he realized he would have been willing to wait for her forever—if she had truly been May Baron and not Dowager Duchess Mary Louise of Lorrania.

Not that his falling in love made a difference. The facts were the same. Her "forever" waited for her back in a small middle European country he'd never heard of before a few days ago. His "forever" was here in the United States. He would do himself a favor if he tried to remember she would be out of his life soon.

All things considered, he told himself as he strode into the foyer to wait for her, maybe it was just as well.

Chapter Five

The following morning Wade had just turned off the shower when the doorbell rang. Dripping wet, he glanced at his waterproof wristwatch. It was only 8:00 a.m., far too early for someone to be leaning on the doorbell. There had to be some mistake.

He was debating taking the time to dress before he answered the door when the doorbell sounded with a series of short rings. A sure sign that whoever was out there was getting impatient. Muttering under his breath, he settled for a towel around his waist and made for the door. What he saw through the peephole made him cuss under his breath and grit his teeth.

To his dismay it was the duchess dressed in an outfit obviously intended to make her look like the average girl next door. Average? Hell, no. Her clothing was a long way from doing the job, but at least she wasn't wearing that garish look-at-me sweat-shirt.

After making sure most of him was hidden from view, he cautiously opened the door. "Your Grace?"

"Yes," she said breathlessly as she glanced over her shoulder. "May I come in?"

Expecting to see the two Secret Service agents, Wade looked behind her. To his dismay, she was alone. Forgetting he wore only a towel, he opened the door and pulled her inside. "Are you okay? Is something wrong? How did you know where I live?"

"One question at a time, please," she answered breathlessly. "You will have to wait until I can catch my breath. I was in a hurry to get here."

"More important," he said after he took another quick look in the hallway and shut the door behind her, "what in heaven's name are you doing here by yourself? Where are Mike and Sam?"

She shrugged as if the Secret Service agents were of no importance. "I saw no reason to include them today."

"You didn't?" he said ominously as he motioned her into the apartment. "Exactly what did you have in mind?"

After yesterday's protest demonstration, Wade had been looking forward to an uneventful day of visiting national monuments—with or without the duchess's enthusiastic cooperation. Instead it looked as if she'd not only ignored his warning that she might be in danger, but his expectations were clearly about to be shot to hell.

What bothered him even more than her unexpected solo appearance was the realization that from the studied smile on her face, the lady was back to trying to do things her way.

She looked luscious and mouthwatering enough in her pale lavender linen pants with a matching mesh linen sweater to please him. She might have looked more like a typical tourist, he thought despairingly, if the see-through sweater had done its job of covering vital parts of her anatomy. Instead the sweater barely concealed a lacy camisole and enough silky skin to make any red-blooded man take notice.

If she was deliberately trying to get his attention, she sure had it.

Clearly, that was the trouble.

What had he ever done to deserve this trial by fire? he wondered uneasily, while he counted to twenty and waited for the duchess to catch her breath. He was a naval officer by choice, and lawyer by training, with an objective and orderly lifestyle. Fairy-tale princesses of fairy-tale countries were something he'd never dreamed of meeting, let alone escorting around D.C....until the duchess came along.

The assignment had started out as official escort duty but was rapidly turning into something more dangerous and, worse yet, more personal. More personal each time they came together, which he didn't care to admit even to himself.

He tried to think of icebergs and snow-capped mountains, but his body wasn't listening to his mind. He tried to remember he was almost naked and had better get some clothes on. When his body hardened under the towel, he knew it was time to get out of sight.

"Chain the door behind you and stay away from the windows," he ordered. "Better yet, don't even move from this room before I come back. Understood, Your Grace?"

She nodded hesitantly. Too hesitantly for Wade's peace of mind.

As he started to turn away, he realized that if he were smart, he would keep the lady too busy to even think of leaving the apartment without him. "Maybe you can make coffee while you wait," he suggested when nothing else of a platonic nature came to mind. When she nodded, he gestured to the small, compact kitchen. "You'll find coffee in the refrigerator. The coffeemaker is over there on the counter.

I'll be back as soon as I shave and dress. We'll talk then.''

May bit her lower lip when Wade spun on his heel and made for a partition that walled off a corner of the room as if the Devil were chasing him. Tall and slender, his muscular nude torso and long athletic legs glistened from a recent shower. Clothed in a towel that covered only his vital parts, she found herself trying to envision him naked in the shower. And herself in there with him. An experience she had never shared with her late husband.

She was surprised and more than a little embarrassed to realize how much she *was* attracted to Wade Stevens. Reluctant bodyguard or not, in or out of uniform, he had a peculiar way of turning her thoughts to forbidden subjects and her body into a bowl of quivering jelly.

She smiled when she heard him mutter to himself and slam drawers before he disappeared into the bathroom. The fact that he was making it clear he wasn't happy to see her didn't bother her. Alone with him, and without the presence of the two un imaginative Secret Service men, this was her only clear chance to persuade Wade to take her around the capital without a disapproving audience.

So far, with the exception of lunch at the Old Post Office and a brief shopping trip in the Capitol Hill District yesterday afternoon, her interesting bodyguard/escort hadn't taken her to any really exciting tourist attractions. The "typical" American lunch of fried chicken and potato salad had been tasty, but she still preferred Mexican cuisine, American or not. The Jefferson Memorial at dusk, while beautiful as promised, hadn't been on her list of must-see destinations.

What she *wanted* to see was Planet Hollywood and the Hard Rock Café—the *in* places she'd read about in a magazine during her air flight to the United States. Or the sights that had been recommended to her by Charlene, "Charlie," Norris, the Blair House concierge. And she had to do it soon.

She had a time crunch, she told herself, to justify her plans. There were only two more days to taste the freedom she yearned for before she returned home to life as a royal puppet. And, according to what her father had indicated, arranged marriage number two.

Her upbringing and her desire to please her father had kept her from rebelling at home. But here, in a free and democratic country, surely she could manage to enjoy herself without the world coming to an end.

She gazed around the large, utilitarian one-room loft apartment. A sofa, an upholstered armchair, a few lamps, a desk and a chair filled one end. Behind the partition at the other end of the room, was what obviously passed as a bedroom. A small kitchen with a counter and bar stools for dining filled the middle of the loft. The only stamp Wade seemed to have put on the apartment appeared to be a stack of books and magazines on a small table. Family pictures of Wade, his parents and his brothers against what seemed like a farming background sat on the desk. A guitar leaned against the armchair.

Compared to her large, richly furnished Baroque suite in Baronovia's royal palace, the loft apartment was pristine and stark, but at least it gave a person room to breathe. Something her rooms in the palace did not. What the apartment lacked, she told herself wistfully, was a woman's touch.

The idea that Wade obviously had no woman in his life gave her food for thought. Maybe *she* could pretend to be that woman, if only for a few days.

She rummaged in the refrigerator for coffee, glanced at the directions on the bag and bit back her frustration. She had never ventured into the palace's kitchen, let alone made coffee. The palace staff would have been demoralized, but how difficult could making a pot of coffee be?

Following the instructions printed on the bag, she carefully measured enough coffee for three cups. One for herself and two for the commander. From the look on his face a few moments ago, he needed it badly. That done, she dropped the ground coffee into the white paper filter she found waiting in the top of the coffeemaker and pushed the plug into the wall. She was jiggling with the coffeemaker's on button with no success when she heard Wade come up behind her.

"It might help if you put in water," he commented dryly. He reached over her shoulder for the glass bottom of the coffeemaker, filled it with three cups of cold water and poured it into the reservoir. In seconds the scent of freshly brewing coffee filled the room.

"Water, of course," May said with a shaky laugh. "What was I thinking?"

"I'm not sure, but I can tell you what I'm thinking." To her surprise Wade turned her around to face him. "You've never made coffee before, have you?"

"No," she answered with a reproachful glance at the coffeemaker. "That is one of the curses of being a member of a wealthy royal family—we do not cook or clean, even if we want to. We have a position to uphold, you understand."

At Wade's raised eyebrows, she went on. "I suppose you could say I have been sheltered from reality, from what you would probably call a normal life. The truth is," she added wistfully, "I would like to feel like a real woman someday."

To her chagrin, Wade's eyebrows rose even higher.

Wade's obvious surprised reaction to her impulsively stated wish to feel like a real woman someday made her blush. Naive and sheltered though she might be, she realized he was bound to think her remark was an invitation. She didn't blame him. It was the last thing she should have said to such a virile man.

Wade eyed her thoughtfully and for a fleeting moment wondered what the duchess had meant by feeling like a real woman. She'd been blunt enough, heaven knew, but the dowager in her title meant she'd been married at one time. Somewhere along the line, surely she must have become a woman.

Deciding discretion was a wiser choice than asking her for an explanation, he chose a safer, alternate route. "I know a few women who aren't that thrilled to cook and clean. They would love to trade places with you."

A frown crinkled her forehead, and her eyes lit up at his attempt to put her at ease, but at least her blush faded. "You do?"

"Sure. My mom and my two sisters-in-law," he added hurriedly before her imagination could run away with her. "All three would kill to be in your shoes. You didn't think I had a harem hidden somewhere in here, did you?"

"Not at all," May said too quickly for her to have meant it, "I was merely curious."

She'd often had the uncomfortable feeling Wade knew what she was thinking before she spoke. Heaven help her, this was one of those times. She avoided his eyes before he sensed she had stopped thinking of him as a bodyguard from the moment he'd opened the apartment door dripping wet and had pulled her inside. To hide her reaction to him, she settled the coffeepot more securely in its holder.

Further disconcerting her, he regarded her with a not-too-subtle expression that sent the butterflies in her middle soaring. To her chagrin, the expression was a look of desire that no man, not even her late husband, had ever shown they felt for her.

She told herself she had to be mistaken. No matter how she felt herself responding to her escort, she had to remember she was a duchess. Wade Stevens's place in her life was merely as her temporary body-guard for the next two days.

She schooled her facial expression and poured freshly brewed coffee into a cup while she forced herself to turn her thoughts to more practical mat-ters. "Cream or sugar?"

"Black, thanks," Wade said. His hand brushed hers as she carefully handed him the cup. She saw a change come over his face as his eyes met hers. Instead of speaking, he frowned, muttered his thanks and turned away. But not before she saw a new awareness of her come into his eyes. An awareness of her as a woman.

Or had she been mistaken?

"I'll take my coffee with me. I only came out to check on you. I still have to shave." Obviously afraid to trust her after she'd evaded the Secret Service agents, he paused. "You *will* be here when I get back?"

"Of course," she said, hoping the look in her eyes didn't register the "maybe" she had planned.

"On the other hand," Wade's voice trailed off as he checked the lock on the door. He looked back at his charge, rubbed the faint stubble on his chin and found himself between a rock and a hard place. He was pretty sure she wouldn't run as soon as he was behind the bathroom door.

On one hand, he could take her with him and have her watch him. On the other hand, he could leave her alone. In the end, it became a case of his common sense taking over.

"Want to join me while I shave? We can talk."

The opportunity to see a man shave, especially *this* man, overcame May's reluctance to put herself where Wade could make further inroads into her senses. It was hard enough to keep from thinking sensuous thoughts when he was clothed, but watching him shave? Imagining him naked under a

shower had been bad enough. And yet…she'd never
even seen a man shave, including her late husband.
The opportunity to watch Wade in action was too
good to pass up. Instead of saying no, she found
herself nodding yes.

He beckoned her into the small bathroom and
pulled out a small wooden stool for her to sit on.

"Comfortable?"

May swallowed hard. The bathroom was still
warm and misty from his shower. All she could
think of was the way Wade must have looked in the
shower with the stream of water pulsating over him.

In the end, May fidgeted on the stool and her body
temperature seemed to go up five degrees. "Yes,"
she managed, "I am fine. Forget I'm here. I do not
wish to bother you."

Wade bit back a blunt remark. He was a red-
blooded American man, dammit. Didn't she realize
she was a desirable woman? How could her presence not bother him in such an intimate setting?

Ordering himself to cool his thoughts, he unbuttoned his shirt, shrugged it off and lathered his face.
A task he undertook almost every day. The trouble
was that today it wasn't easy. Not when he could
see her reflection in the mirror raptly watching each
stroke of the razor. To add to his problems, she
looked like the sundae she'd ordered yesterday at

the Old Post Office. Creamy, soft and undoubtedly delicious.

Heaven help him, he muttered when he nicked his chin for the third time and had to reach for another piece of tissue to stop the tiny flow of blood. No matter how hard he'd tried to forget the delectable duchess was inches away from him, he was in a no-win situation. At the rate he was going, he muttered to himself, he'd probably wind up cutting his throat.

May was fascinated as she watched Wade shave. She hadn't realized there would be something so sensual in the way the razor slid across his handsome face, first up and then down. Or how his muscles undulated with his movements. Her fingers itched to caress the tanned, smooth skin on his face left in the razor's wake, to sooth away the sting of the tiny cuts he made on his chin.

Heaven help her, there was even something sexy about the way he glanced at her through the mirror. And in the way he paused to swallow the hot, black coffee he had brought into the room with him. By the time she realized she couldn't take much more of watching him at the very masculine and sensual task of shaving, even her toes were tingling.

Tissue-covered cuts and all, Wade Stevens was a very sexy man.

But now that she saw the physical difference between her late husband and Wade, that was not all that troubled her. The intimate scene reminded her of what she had been missing in her proper and arranged marriage to an older man who had avoided any kind of intimacy. A man who had lived behind a closed door at one end of their suite. To add to her unhappiness, her husband had been more of a polite visitor to her bedroom than a welcome lover.

She caught herself thinking of what life would have been like if she'd been simply May Baron. Or if she'd been married to a man like Wade Stevens and lived in a loft apartment such as this one. His face would have been the last one she would see before she fell asleep at night and the first one she would see when she awakened in the morning instead of a uniformed maid bearing a cup of hot chocolate.

She would have been more than happy to learn to cook for such a man. To add feminine touches to the loft; to make it a home. To be the woman he kissed goodbye in the morning and came home to at night. As for making love… She realized with a shock that she'd never thought of her marital relationship with her late husband as making love.

Futile dreams, she told herself. Nothing had changed. She was Mary Louise, Dowager Duchess of Lorrania. She had to remember all that that entailed, before she allowed her imagination to run away with her. And to remember that the last place she should find herself was in a tiny bathroom watching Wade shave.

She wanted to stay, but there was a problem. While her bodyguard might want to keep an eye on her, she couldn't trust herself to keep her eyes off him.

"Er, I think I'll go get my coffee," she finally managed as she edged her way out of the too-warm bathroom. "If you do not mind, I will wait for you outside."

"Promise?" He didn't sound as if he believed he would find her there when he was finished shaving.

"Promise," she echoed as she edged around Wade and out the door.

May waited until she heard the bathroom door close behind her before she headed for the pitcher of ice water she'd seen in the refrigerator. If she couldn't cool her thoughts, at least she could cool off her body.

Chapter Six

May was sipping coffee and trying to keep her mind off the mental picture of Wade shaving when she heard a knock at the door. Mindful of Wade's warning, she went to peer through the peephole.

To her surprise, Serge Antonov, a member of her father's entourage, stood on the other side of the door. The man was big and burly and had dark black hair, bushy black eyebrows and dark-brown eyes. Although threatening in appearance, he was still a man who had been her father's bodyguard for eight years. A man she'd always considered a friend to her and her family.

After a tentative glance at the closed bathroom door, she slipped open the locks. "Yes?"

"At your service, Your Grace," he said with a courtesy nod. "His Highness is downstairs in his limousine and would like to speak to you for a few moments."

Now what? May hesitated and glanced at the bathroom door. She'd promised Wade she would remain in the apartment, but her father's wishes were just as important to her, maybe even more. Gazing at the man's dark-brown eyes, she began to wish she hadn't answered the door.

"I left no word where I was going, Serge. How did you know where to find me?"

"I identified myself to the concierge at the Blair House as your father's bodyguard. I told the lady that His Highness wished to speak to you and to see for himself that you are well. It was then that she told me you'd left to join the commander, Your Grace."

May hesitated in the doorway, the hairs on the back of her neck prickling. Something about the man's demeanor was not right. "I don't understand, Serge. I am here with my American bodyguard, Commander Stevens. Surely my father trusts the commander to see to me?"

The frowning man shrugged his huge shoulders. "I am merely doing my duty, Your Grace. His Highness is waiting for you downstairs and has asked me to tell you he will keep you for only a few moments. Please come with me."

Afraid to break her promise to remain in the apartment, May hesitated and glanced at the bathroom door. Her father's wishes and his peace of mind were as important to her as her promise to Wade. If she hurried, she would be back before Wade realized she was gone.

"Very well. I will come with you." She glanced at the clock on the wall and swept out the door. Her father's bodyguard followed, but not before he carefully and quietly closed the apartment door behind her.

"Your Grace? May?" Wade came out of the bathroom wiping his face clean of shaving soap. A swift glance around the room told him the loft was empty. In spite of her promise to stay put, May had flown the coop.

It was his fault, he muttered as threw the towel on the bed behind him. He should have known the lady was the last person he could trust. And that one way or another she intended to have things go her way.

He grabbed a fresh shirt, ready to go after May. And when he found her, he promised himself, he would read her the riot act and take her back to the Blair House for someone else to worry about her.

Until he noticed her straw bag on the couch. Her half-full coffee cup was on the counter, still steaming. From the looks of things, she had to have expected to return soon. Something was wrong! His senses told him May was in some kind of danger. And not just from rotten vegetables.

Whatever or whoever had prompted her to leave the apartment had to have taken place no more than a few moments ago. If he hurried, maybe he could still catch up with her.

Without stopping to think rationally, he grabbed his holster and loaded his Beretta out of a desk drawer and took the stairs three at a time to the street. To his horror he saw the duchess being forced into a limo by the same dark-haired man he'd noticed skulking around the National Portrait Gallery yesterday. She was hollering her head off and putting up a stiff fight, but it was evident she was no match for her would-be abductor. With a curse Wade pulled the Beretta from its holster and made for the limo.

"Stop! Stop right there!" he shouted as he ran, his gun held in both hands and prepared to shoot as soon as he had a clear target. And, even then, he remembered not to give May's identity away. "Let the woman go before I shoot!"

Behind him a woman pedestrian shrieked. "Help, police! The man has a gun!"

It took Wade a split second to realize the woman was talking about him. The fact that May was being abducted hadn't seemed to register.

Wade didn't stop to identify himself. By the time he did, May would have been long gone.

"I have a cell phone. I'll call 911!" another voice

shouted. A passing car burned rubber as the driver trod on the gas in an attempt to get out of the line of fire.

If Wade had hoped for help in rescuing May, the idea died a quick death. With the bystanders milling around, bumping into each other and getting nowhere, saving May was strictly up to him.

His immediate problem was that, as much as he wanted to shoot the bastard who had May in a neck hold, he couldn't. Not without taking the chance he might hit some innocent bystander or, heaven forbid, May herself.

The kidnapper struggled to push May, a whirlwind of arms and legs, into the limo. To Wade's fervent approval, she kneed her attacker where it would hurt him the most, then bit his hand. After a second kick her attacker shoved her down to the pavement. With a fierce growl and a foul oath, he threw himself into the limo in time for it to take off with the passenger door open.

Wade paused only long enough to help May struggle to her feet.

"Are you going to be okay?" he asked, hurriedly searching her body for possible injuries.

"Yes," she said breathlessly.

Wade nodded and ran after the limo that was about to skid around the corner. He took aim and fired at its rear tires, but it was too late. Too late to even get the license number, probably a fake anyway, he muttered as he ran back to May, helped her up and put his arms around her. ''Are you sure you're all right?''

She shivered in his arms and her eyes were glazed—both sure signs she was on the verge of shock. With a curse, he drew back to make sure she hadn't been hurt. She had no visible wounds, but her chin and her neck, where her would-be captor had held her in a choke hold, were turning black and blue. Her elbows, where she'd scraped her skin after being thrown to the pavement, were raw and bleeding. The see-through sweater was almost torn from her shoulders.

To Wade's mind, she was far from okay and needed immediate attention. His frustration and his fear for her fueled his anger. ''Why in the hell didn't you stay upstairs like you promised?''

After realizing May was in no condition to answer, he swallowed the rest of his questions and carried her back to his apartment. He'd intended to remind her in no uncertain terms that her life had been in danger, clean her up and take her home. Instead he found himself tenderly holding her in his arms as if she were fragile and might break. And wishing he could somehow kiss away the bruises on her cheek and on her neck.

Behind him, he heard a man shout, ''The cops are

on their way!'' Wade shuddered when he heard police sirens in the distance. Hell, he thought as he gathered May closer into his arms and made for his apartment. The last thing he needed was a gaggle of policemen asking questions he had sworn to keep secret. As far as he was concerned, the State Department and the D.C. police could fight it out without his help.

"You won't let the police arrest me, will you?" May whispered brokenly into his shoulder. "I do not want to embarrass my father or my country."

"No, Your Grace. They won't arrest you. You haven't done anything wrong. Besides you have diplomatic immunity," he said as he strode up the stairs. Even though he knew duty required him to call her father and to inform the State Department about May's whereabouts and the morning's events, he couldn't do it. Not when May was so obviously afraid they would find out. "And I won't tell your father," he added. "Not if you don't want me to."

"Not yet, perhaps later," she answered. "But what if the police find us and try to question me? What shall I tell them?"

"No problem. Like I said, you can claim diplomatic immunity. If that doesn't hold them off, I'll think of something. I'm a lawyer, remember?" He pushed open the door to his apartment and, balancing her with one arm, carefully double locked the door behind him. Safe in the apartment, he placed her on the couch and drew a deep breath of relief. So far, so good, but he sensed their troubles were far from over.

"Hang on. I'll be right back." He went to the refrigerator, shook some ice cubes into a towel and came back to gently hold the towel to her bruised cheek. "Mind telling me what that was all about?"

"I'm not sure," she answered. She gazed up at him and covered his hand with one of her own. Tears formed at the corner of her eyes. "I've known Serge for eight years. He is one of my father's bodyguards and, I thought, my friend. Why would he want to harm me?"

Wade's anger melted at the touch of May's cold hand on his. His guilt at not having protected her warred with his instincts to hold her in his arms. To kiss her and swear to keep her safe forever.

But "forever" was only two more days.

He felt his blood run cold at the obvious answer to her question about her father's bodyguard. Throughout history, more than one bodyguard had been paid to assassinate his employer. Unfortunately, today's scenario sounded more of the same. Someone out there didn't want to see Prince Alexis or see any member of his family remain on the throne. And that included May.

He pulled out his cell phone and spoke tersely into it.

"Are you angry with me?"

"Yes," he answered. Now was as good a time as any to tell the truth. "I'm more angry with myself. I should have realized you were in danger, even here with me."

She took the ice pack away from her cheek and winced. "I must apologize for causing you so much trouble. It will not happen again."

"Deal." He gazed down at her with a smile that broke her heart. In that moment he was no longer Commander Wade Stevens of the United States Navy. He could not have known it, but he was fast becoming her fairy-tale prince.

"There's a first-aid kit in the bathroom. I'll be right back, sweetheart."

"Sweetheart?" She echoed faintly.

Wade wanted to bite his tongue. Compassion was fine. So was empathy for her tangled situation. Hadn't he already told himself that calling her a term of endearment was definitely not in order. It was his turn to apologize.

"Sorry if I was too familiar, Your Grace. I'm afraid I got carried away in the heat of the moment." He rose and stood gazing down at her in time to see her face, bruises and all, turn a becoming pink.

"Would you call me sweetheart if I were really May?" she asked.

He nodded reluctantly. Their relationship, begun as a lark on her part, had turned serious. When had she managed to worm her way into his heart? When had he realized the woman he'd considered a pain in the neck had become his pain in the neck?

"*If* you were only May," he said carefully. "But we both know you're more than that, don't we?"

"Yes, I am afraid I do," she answered. Her eyes spoke of her regret before they turned enigmatic. When the light went out of her eyes, it damn near broke his heart. "Of course you are right, Commander."

"Call me Wade, Your Grace," he said as he brushed her bruised cheek with gentle fingers. "As for what I have to call you—in public, you can pretend to be May. In here, I'm afraid you'll have to be the duchess—for both of our sakes. Agreed?"

"Agreed." She echoed softly. To his regret he caught a glimpse of sadness come back into her eyes.

A pounding at the door stopped him in his tracks. The D.C. police? He motioned the duchess into silence and checked the peephole. Thank God, his visitors were the two Secret Service agents assigned to the duchess.

"Where in the hell have you been?" he growled

as he threw open the door. "I would have thought your absence the other day would have taught you guys something."

"We were only gone for a few moments, and only because we were chasing a shady character," Mike Wheeler replied through tight lips. "And, yeah, it taught us something," he added with a cool glance at the duchess. "What's damn clear is that the lady can't be trusted. Good thing you called and verified she's was here with you."

"Verified?"

His partner, Sam, broke in. "Yeah. We already knew where the duchess was. Charlie Norris, the concierge back at the Blair House, told us she felt sorry for the duchess and gave her your address. From the way Mike and I heard the scam," he added sourly, "it sounded as if the duchess here, is able to charm the birds right out of their nests."

"Charlie also told us some big guy said he was the prince's bodyguard and was looking for the duchess," Mike Wheeler added. "Come to think of it, it sounded like it was the same guy we were chasing at the National Gallery yesterday. We got over here as fast as we could, but from the looks of things out there on the street, we weren't fast enough."

Wade heard footsteps thundering up the stairs. He quickly filled the agents in with the earlier attempted kidnapping of the duchess. "We can't let anyone know the truth of what went on, at least not yet," he added when a voice outside the door shouted, "Police! Open up in there!"

Mike took over. "Let me handle this." He opened the door. Four members of the D.C. police stood there, hands on their holsters.

"Anything wrong, officers?"

"There's been a shooting, sir. Witnesses downstairs directed us here. We have a few questions we need to ask. With your permission, we'd like to come inside." The lead officer glanced over Mike's shoulder at Wade. His head swiveled to the couch. "From the description two witnesses gave us, I'd say that's the man who shot off a gun. And the lady over there on the couch looks like the woman who was the target of all the action."

Mike pulled out his identification and showed it to the officers. "Official business, Officer. We have everything in hand."

"Official or not," the officer reluctantly conceded after a glance at Mike's badge. "We can't have people shooting guns on city streets. Hell, we could have had a riot on our hands!"

Mike shot Wade a warning glance before he could protest. "Like I said, Officer. We have everything in hand."

The officer nodded reluctantly and studied the duchess. "Looks as if the lady needs some medical attention. Maybe we ought to call an ambulance and take her to the hospital.''

"Nothing we can't handle right here, Officer," Mike replied. He motioned for the police to leave. "It won't happen again."

Wade silently watched the uniformed men leave. Agent Wheeler might want to believe there wouldn't be any more trouble involving the duchess, but he had his doubts. Intentionally or not, trouble seemed to have a way of finding her. And, ever since he'd been appointed her escort/bodyguard, it seemed to find him as well.

He raked his fingers through his damp hair and turned back to the apartment. "May, I am your bodyguard, but I don't think I can take any more of this. The fact is, sweetheart, you've just taken ten years off my life."

May's eyes warmed at the term of endearment and the mention of her nickname. The Secret Service agents glanced at each other.

Wade cleared his throat when the silence became obvious. "Sorry about that, Your Grace. I guess I shouldn't have said that. I'm afraid the stress of the morning got to me."

She was back to being the duchess. It didn't seem to matter how they were beginning to feel about each other. May inclined her head. "I understand,

Commander. It is I who should apologize for causing the stress.''

"Commander, I think we need to talk," Agent Wheeler interjected and motioned to the hall. His partner snorted his agreement.

Wade knew all too well what they wanted to talk about—his out-of-bounds familiarity with the duchess.

Hell, hadn't he "talked" to himself on the same subject ever since he'd found out the identity of the beautiful lady in white?

And once he'd found out her identity, hadn't he told himself wanting her, or even allowing himself to care for her, was an exercise in futility?

Hadn't he already reminded himself he was a guy from a small town in Nebraska who had gotten lucky when his congressman had sponsored him for the naval academy?

And hadn't he reminded himself the woman he was falling in love with was far out of reach for a man like him?

Bottom line, the last thing he needed at this point in his ten-year career was to cause an international incident.

"We'd like to have a few private words with you, Commander," Mike Wheeler repeated.

Wade winced when he heard the ominous tone in the agent's voice. As if he didn't have enough trouble on his hands, he'd added a possible breach of conduct to his list of stupidity.

The list was already too long.

Number one on the list was that he'd broken a cardinal rule for bodyguards: he'd gotten emotionally involved with his charge.

He gestured helplessly to the loft apartment. "I'm afraid there's no room for a private talk in here. If it's going to be just the three of us, I guess we could step out into the hall for a minute." He looked back over his shoulder and shrugged. "Her Grace can't possibly get into any more trouble with the three of us right outside the door."

If only he could believe it. If only it didn't appear as if trouble, in one way or another, was the duchess's middle name. And if only he hadn't fallen like a ton of bricks for May.

The private "talk" over and the Secret Service agents out of earshot downstairs, Wade sank onto the couch besides May. Determined to somehow end the growing and impossible relationship between them before it was too late, he steeled himself to speak. "Your Grace, I…"

"One moment, please," she said, proudly. She put a staying finger across his lips. "I suspect I know what you are going to say, but I cannot allow you to say it. Not now, and certainly not before I explain my behavior."

"There was no need to explain," Wade said ruefully after May told him about her arranged marriage and her desire to be herself for the few days she was in the United States. "For that matter, I haven't behaved too well myself. I have a lot to apologize for. I should have found a way to convince you of the dangers you face without being so forceful."

"Perhaps you were overly anxious about my welfare," May replied. "However, it seems you were correct and I was wrong. I find it difficult to believe, but obviously I am in danger."

"Unfortunately, that's true, Your Grace. It certainly brings home who and what you are."

Her expression turned bleak when he reverted to being formal. He couldn't help himself. Addressing May by her title was the only way he could keep his emotional distance. The expression on her face damn near broke his heart. It was going to get a lot worse when she heard his next move, but he'd made up his mind. He was going to ask to be taken off the assignment as her bodyguard—for both their sakes.

It was more for her good than his, he told himself. May was entitled to someone's undivided impersonal attention, not a man who was fast becoming interested in his charge in all the ways a man is drawn to a desirable woman.

He clenched his fists until his fingernails bit into

his flesh. He had to remind himself that as much as he wanted to take May in his arms and make love to her, she was off-limits.

So much for falling in love for the first time in his life.

And yet, even as he steeled himself to say good-bye, the look that passed over her eyes touched a place in his heart he hadn't known was there.

He took her hand and pulled her into his arms. To comfort her, he told himself. Only to comfort her for a few moments before he would go back to being her bodyguard and she Duchess Mary Louise.

He'd planned on asking for a change of assignment, but now he realized he wanted to stay and protect her. At least for the remaining two days before she walked out of his life forever.

His fate was sealed when she turned her face up to his and a yearning look came into her eyes. In a heartbeat she was no longer the duchess, he was no longer the man designated to protect her from harm. They became a man and a woman hovering on the brink of a wonderful discovery.

There was only one thing a man falling in love for the first time could do.

He kissed her.

Chapter Seven

May kissed him back. Instead of the hesitant kiss he'd expected, there was an urgency about her response that took him by surprise—the urgency of an awakened woman. How she could have endured a loveless marriage when she had such fire in her? he wondered as he deepened his kiss.

"May," he whispered as he tenderly held her face between his hands and sought more of her honeyed lips. The taste of her, the sound of her quickened breath and the way she melted into his arms told him how much she wanted him. Her need somehow lessened part of his conscience.

When she sighed with contentment, he went on to brush her flushed skin with his tongue, caress the nape of her neck and the hollow between her breasts. When she murmured her pleasure, he slid her sweater off her shoulders and kissed his way down her silken skin.

It was the pounding of her heart against his lips that awakened him to the dangerous road they were taking. A road he would be foolish to enter and from which there could be no turning back.

No matter how much he wished that the world outside the door to his apartment would disappear, it was still out there waiting for him. He'd already been warned by the two Secret Service agents he was violating his duty by showing how much he cared for the precious woman in his arms?

With his thoughts spinning wildly, he held May close and took a deep breath to calm his own heart.

How could he make love to May today knowing there would be no tomorrows for them?

How could he make love to her knowing that saying goodbye was all there was for them after the gala farewell ball tomorrow night?

How could he be the one to break her heart one more time?

"May," he said when he finally had his body under control, "we have to stop." He caught himself before he forgot himself and called her sweetheart again. This time, it would have been for real. "We have to remember we have no future together. Your life is back in Baronovia. Mine is here. I can't betray the trust our governments have placed in me."

"For now, all I want is here," she whispered,

clutching his shoulders. "I do not want to think of tomorrow—only of the next few moments. Until now I've been a possession. Now I want to know how it feels to be a whole woman."

Like a magnet, the stars in her eyes threatened to draw him back to her embrace. But just as duty, honor and country were engraved in his conscious as an officer in the United States Navy, the same duty and honor kept him from taking advantage of her obvious vulnerability.

He gently drew her torn sweater back over her shoulders. "I'm sorry, but just as you said you couldn't live without explaining yourself, I couldn't live with myself if I weren't honest with you."

"Wade," she whispered, longing shining from her eyes. "I want..."

"I know," he answered, "but we have to stop before it's too late." He gently pulled her torn sweater back over her breasts. "These few days we have together can only be make-believe. No matter how you think you now feel, you deserve more than this."

She wiped away the tears that spilled out of the corners of her eyes. "Is it because you do not care for me, or is it because we are from two different worlds?"

"Two different worlds and centuries apart." Unable to tell her much he had come to care for her and still be able to let her go, he agreed to the half-truth.

The light in her eyes faded. To his regret the May he'd fallen in love with vanished before his eyes. And in her place she was the Dowager Duchess of Lorrania. Cool, reserved and untouchable.

He wanted to take her in his arms and tell her he hadn't meant to hurt her. He ached to tell her he had fallen in love with her, but honor kept him from telling her so.

He took a deep breath, gently put May away from him and rose to his feet. He hated himself for hurting her and knew he had to do something to take the sadness out of her eyes. His thoughts spun over possibilities until he realized the only way he could lessen the sexual tension between them was to make sure they would never be alone again for the rest of her stay.

"I think it's probably a good idea to get out of here for a while," he said into her silence. "I'll call some friends to join us for the afternoon. In the meantime, why don't you freshen up?"

May glanced down at her torn sweater and grimaced. "I can hardly go out looking like this. I might attract attention."

She was right, Wade realized as his body warmed. She would never be able to keep a low profile with bare, creamy shoulders and a lacy bra that revealed more than it should have.

"No problem. I have a shirt you can borrow." Wade went to his closet and slipped a fresh white shirt from its hanger. "It's way too large, but if you tie it around your waist you'll be in style."

May took the shirt and went into the bathroom to change. Once out of Wade's sight, she buried her face in his shirt and let her emotions take over.

For the first time in her life she had been tempted to forget who she was. And for the first time she hadn't cared about the consequences of her actions. Until now, she'd lived in a gilded prison, and no matter what Wade has said about the future, she still yearned to be free. To be May Baron, if only for a few days.

How could she tell him her brief, married years had left her yearning for something she sensed was waiting for her out there but had been out of her reach? If she couldn't have had a husband who loved her, at least she'd hoped for children of her own to cherish and to love. Instead, her husband had treated her like a stranger, had slept with her as if it had been a duty. And, to further break her heart, she had remained childless.

She gazed into the mirror and saw the reflection of her sad eyes, the streaks of dried tears on her cheeks and her disheveled hair. Instead of being a

woman to be pitied, surely it was time to take matters into her own hands. She intended to fight for
the few precious hours of freedom, as well as the
moments of sexual abandon she yearned for. If she
were going to experience the romantic interlude with
Wade, it would have to be up to her.

She would let tomorrow take care of itself.

She washed her face, undid her chignon and
brushed her hair with Wade's brush until it lay
freely around her shoulders. The shirt he had given
her was too large, but she deliberately tied it high
under her breasts leaving bare a wide expanse of
skin.

Gazing at herself in the mirror, she was satisfied
at the change in her. She no longer looked like the
duchess she had been from birth. She might not be
simply May Baron, but surely she resembled some
of the other young women she'd seen laughing on
the streets of Washington.

By the time she was through with Wade, she intended to make him forget who she was. And to
have him treat her as the real woman she was inside.
It was her one chance at happiness, and she intended
to take it.

IF HE'D THOUGHT being surrounded by company
would keep his mind off May, one look at her told
him he'd been wrong. As for his duty as her body-

guard, Wade knew it was going to be harder than it had been before.

He and May made their way downstairs and into the noonday sunshine. To his dismay, pedestrians still lingered outside, pointing to the building and babbling about the near kidnapping. To avoid being questioned, he quickly drew May down the street.

His fellow JAG lawyer, Daniel O'Hara, the friend he'd called to keep him out of trouble, was waiting on the corner in company of the two Secret Service agents. After seeing the admiring look that came over Dan's face and the faces of the agents when they caught a glimpse of May, Wade knew he was not only not out of trouble, he was jealous. Jealous not only of Dan, but of every man whose eyes lit up when they lingered on May. Secret Service included.

As requested, Dan was dressed in civilian clothing. The only problem was that, in or out of uniform, Dan resembled a well-known movie star—all six feet three inches of him. Now that he had a chance to think clearly, Wade realized that his blond and blue-eyed friend was probably the last man he should have invited to keep his own thoughts away from May. Not when Dan had a killer smile and a happy-go-lucky persona to go with it. And not when he'd already sensed May had a trick or two left up her sleeve.

Wade took a deep breath, hoped for the best and plunged into introductions.

"Your Grace, I'd like you to meet Daniel O'Hara, a fellow officer of mine. Dan, this is Duchess Mary Louise of Lorrania. The duchess is visiting D.C. for a few days."

May smiled and held out her hand. "I am pleased to meet you. Please call me May."

Dan looked at Wade and raised an inquiring eyebrow. At Wade's nod, Dan took May's hand and grinned happily. "Sure, if you call me Dan."

When May dimpled, Agent Mike Wheeler cleared his throat. "Why don't we all get in the car and get moving." He gestured to an unmarked black sedan waiting at the curb. "Where to, Commander?"

"Georgetown," Wade said with a warning frown at Dan. "I hear there's a great ice-cream parlor near Wisconsin and M."

"Ice-cream parlor?" Dan sounded incredulous. "I thought we were going to show May D.C."

"May likes ice-cream sundaes." When her eyes widened in pleased surprise, Wade knew that if he wanted to keep an impersonal note between them, he'd just made a big mistake. How was he going to keep their relationship on an impersonal level if he kept remembering endearing things about his charge? "We're meeting someone there."

The someone turned out to be Charlene Norris,

who had recommended the ice-cream parlor as a place to keep May safe and out of sight for now. Knowing the way May and trouble traveled in pairs, he wasn't so sure.

With Mike Wheeler and Sam Hoskins seated at a small wrought iron table near the door, Wade introduced the newcomer. "May, this is Charlene, concierge at the Blair House. Charlene's offered to show you a side of D.C. she thinks you might want to see."

"Call me Charlie," the smiling newcomer told May. "From what Wade told me on the telephone, I gather you want to keep your identity hidden and fade into the city's landscape, right?"

"Right," May echoed, fascinated by the informal aura that clung to Charlie. And because it would serve no purpose to reveal that Charlie was the one who had given away the location of Wade's apartment, she kept her silence. "I have never heard of a woman called Charlie before. Does it present a problem?"

"None that I can't handle," Charlie answered with a mischievous grin. "You might even say it's an icebreaker."

Wade noticed Dan rolling his eyes at Charlie's comment. Dan liked his women short and feminine. Especially when their midriff was showing and their slacks hung low on finely contoured hips. The idea that he'd asked Dan along to help him keep his mind off May became more and more ridiculous with each admiring glance Dan gave her.

To complicate matters for Wade, not even the chatter of the effervescent Charlie Norris could take Wade's mind off May. Not when her quaint way of speech and the shirt tied high under her breasts were driving him to distraction.

Bottom line, he had to be twice as watchful, three times as objective and ten times more determined to keep his mind off May in order to see himself through the next two days.

In sharp contrast to May, Charlie Norris was a tall, slender brunette who knew half of Washington's elite by their first name. Employed by the State Department to ease the stay of visiting dignitaries, she was not only streetwise, she had a mind that was an encyclopedia of knowledge she was known to put to good use. And, in view of her happy-go-lucky attitude, was probably skating on the outer edge of her employer's approval.

Just as he was skating the State Department's disapproval for allowing himself to become emotionally involved with the duchess.

And just as he knew the two Secret Service men had been admonished for their lack of attention to the safety of their charge.

At least it was comforting to know that they all had something in common.

It was only going to be a matter of time before this morning's near-miss kidnapping became newspaper headline material. For sure, Undersecretary Logan was bound to make good his threat to remove Wade as May's bodyguard if anything else happened.

It had been another reason he'd hurried May out of his apartment before official orders came to take her back to the Blair House. No matter what he'd told himself, he wasn't ready to give her up.

Wade took in May's petite form, made unusually eye-catching by the slacks that rode low on her hips and the shirt that left her smooth, flat stomach showing. Her chestnut hair, which she usually wore in a severe chignon at the nape of her neck, now flowed freely about her face. She might have looked like a May, but he would still do well to remember the way she looked now was just a charade.

To add to her American-girl appearance, somewhere in the past hour of sight-seeing and shopping along the picturesque streets of Georgetown, she'd managed to find a pair of barefoot sandals that were anchored on her delicate feet by a single strap between her slender toes, with their brightly colored toenails. To add to her new appearance, a chunky chain of inexpensive gemstones hung around her ankle. She even wore rings on her toes.

He would have bet the farm that even though she drew second glances, no one could possibly have recognized May's true identity. Maybe he *didn't* have to worry about her safety any longer.

He shook his head to clear it. He still had the uneasy feeling she was plotting something. And from the innocent glances she kept sending his way, he sure as heck had to be the victim of her plans. Why else was she making sure he noticed her?

Like a sedate caterpillar, Duchess Mary Louise had metamorphosed into a colorful butterfly no real man could help notice...or resist.

He wanted to grab her, march her to a secluded spot and kiss the truth out of her. If the something she was scheming was going to be an iffy proposition, he intended to know about it in advance. Furthermore, he intended to keep one step ahead of her and make sure she wasn't planning to shake off him or the Secret Service.

"Something on your mind?" Dan asked.

"Why?" Wade glanced behind him to where May and Charlie had joined tourists in admiring hand-painted silk scarves offered by a sidewalk salesman.

"Maybe because you were muttering to yourself."

Wade wiped a hand across his forehead and shook his head. "It's a long story. Bottom line, things are a mess."

"By 'mess' I assume you're speaking of the little lady back there?"

"Yep," Wade answered with a jaundiced glance at the sidewalk vendor and the man's growing audience. "Who else?"

Dan laughed. "The two Secret Service guys back there trying to look inconspicuous don't look too happy about the lady, either."

Wade grinned wryly when he checked out Mike and Sam's uncomfortable body language. "You wouldn't feel at home admiring outrageous rhinestone sunglasses either if you'd been trained to shoot first and ask questions later."

Dan shrugged. "So, tell me again how you became the duchess's bodyguard?"

"I was invited to one official cocktail party too many, that's how."

Dan raised an eyebrow. "That simple?"

"Simple? Hell no," Wade ground out. "It started out that way, but it's gotten complicated as hell."

"Nice complication, if you ask me." Dan glanced admiringly at May. "Damn nice."

"You wouldn't think so if you knew there hasn't been a peaceful moment from the time she and I were introduced."

Dan tore his eyes away from May and studied his friend. "Sounds as if the lady has gotten under your skin. So what's the problem?"

"In a nutshell—she's not available."

"You must have known that from the start, friend. So why not go with the attraction?"

Frustrated, Wade raked his fingers through his hair. "Maybe because there hasn't been a dull moment with May around. Before that, between growing up on a farm and serving in the military, my life was pretty predictable."

"Maybe that's why you're so attracted to her— you're tired of the predictable. Maybe you were ready for a little spice to your life."

Before Wade could finish telling Dan the whole story, Charlie bounded up, with May following at a more sedate pace. They each carried newly purchased Frisbees, and to his mounting dismay, it looked as if they intended to use them. Between May's risqué costume and an attention-getting activity like throwing Frisbees, how were they going to remain inconspicuous?

"Come on, Wade, Dan! May and I have decided to go over to Georgetown Park," Charlie announced happily. "It's going to be the two of us against the two of you!"

"Grow up," Dan growled with a cautious glance

at the Frisbees. "I've never thrown one of those in my life."

"Time you learned," Charlie insisted. "May says she's willing to learn, why not you?"

From the pleased look on May's face, Wade didn't doubt she was ready, willing and able to go along with any idea Charlie came up with. Any more than he doubted that he and Dan were going to be on the losing side of any contest they entered into with them. "Are you sure you want to throw Frisbees, May?"

She smiled at him. "As long as I am here in your country I would like to learn to play like an American woman."

Fried chicken and potato salad, Mexican food and now Frisbees, Wade mused as he found himself returning her smile; all harmless enough. If throwing Frisbees made her happy, it was okay with him. "Why not?"

Over the mutterings of the two Secret Service agents, they found themselves in Georgetown Park warming up before starting a game. It was him and Dan against Charlie and May. Mike and Sam stood on the sidelines keeping cautious eyes on the surrounding territory.

The brilliant sunshine and the happy shouts of contestants filled the air as they hurtled the multicolored Frisbees.

He couldn't remember seeing May as happy as she appeared to be this moment. Gone were the royal constraints. In their place rang her carefree laughter as she ran with abandon and cheered her partner on.

The rough-and-tumble game of seeing how far they each could throw a Frisbee and have it return to the proper sender almost took Wade's mind off any sensual thoughts involving May. But not quite.

"You're pretty good at this for an amateur," he told her when she laughingly handed him his Frisbee. "Considering."

"I used to play handball with a cousin," she answered smugly over her shoulder in passing.

He tried harder. No wonder she was whiz at Frisbee. His game had been touch football. Maybe it should have been handball.

The next thing he knew May slammed into him while running backward in an attempt to catch her Frisbee.

Instinctively he threw out his arms to catch her, overbalanced, and they both wound up falling together on the grass. By the time he was able to untangle himself, they were both laughing...until he found himself eyeball to eyeball, nose to nose and hip to hip with the woman he'd almost decided to distance himself from.

The contact between them pressed his Beretta into

his chest. That reminder that he was May's body-guard should have cooled the way he felt about her. Instead, all he could think of at the moment was how wonderful she felt in his arms.

Maybe it was the look that came into her eyes as her laughter faded. A powerful awareness of their proximity took over, and he found himself staring down at her lips.

Her eyes widened and her lips parted. Breathless, grass-stained, and with her silken hair flowing over her forehead, May was even more appealing now than the woman she'd been when he'd held her in his arms. Earlier, he'd seen the dawning awareness of sexual attraction between them growing in her eyes. Now her exotic green eyes not only sparkled with laughter, her lips seemed to beg to be kissed. Her arms tightened around him. Even as their gazes locked, he felt his body responding.

He wanted to kiss her smiling mouth, which was only inches away from his own. He wanted to kiss the corners of her exotic eyes. To slide his hands over her shoulders, her bare midriff and even her tantalizing breasts. Heaven help him, he wanted to tell her he'd actually gone beyond being attracted to her. To tell her he'd fallen in love with every de-lectable inch of her.

"Need any help?"

Wade grimaced at the suggestive tone in Dan's

voice. The sexual tension between himself and May remained. To his chagrin, he remembered his father's favorite expression: a lesson unlearned is a lesson doomed to be repeated.

Wade drew a deep breath and glanced up at his friend. Dan's knowing look and the sight of the two Secret Service men loping his way washed over Wade like a bucket of cold water.

How could he have been stupid enough to wind up on the grass in a public park with his arms wrapped around the duchess of Lorrania? And after he'd made an iron-clad pledge to himself to keep his distance from her?

Or, more intriguingly, had May run into him deliberately?

And what was behind the look in her eyes?

He motioned Dan away, jumped to his feet and offered May his hand. "No, thanks. We're okay." He looked to May for confirmation. To his mounting dismay, she smiled.

"I'd say you're both doing great," Dan murmured as he covertly gestured to the Secret Service agents who'd halted a few yards away. "But if I were you, I'd cool it until you're someplace private."

Private? The word held all the connotations of things Wade had convinced himself he'd been trying to avoid. If anything proved he'd been fooling himself it was his reaction to his tumble onto the grass with May.

Another of his father's favorite sayings came to mind: The road to hell is paved with good intentions. If his father was right, and it sure looked as if he was, he knew himself to be only inches away from the edge of that road.

"Thanks a bunch," he muttered before he rescued May's sandal. "Sorry for getting in your way," he told her. "Are you sure you're okay?"

"I am fine," she answered with a winsome expression. Those intriguing dimples danced in her cheeks. She held out a foot and stared at it doubtfully. "I am afraid the sandals weren't made for running."

Wade glanced down at May's bare feet. He was holding one of her sandals and the other was hanging from her ankle by its strap. Her feet were streaked with green grass stains, but, thank God, all ten toes looked in working order.

He swallowed hard. He'd never been a foot man, but even May's pink toenails were actually flirting with him. He helped her take the broken sandal off her foot and put the sandals into his jacket pocket. "No problem. We'll buy you a new pair as soon as we're through here."

"I am unaccustomed to playing like this, you understand,'' May said with an apologetic smile. "In my country, a duchess doesn't play ball in public."

Wade thought of his own childhood, when he, his brothers and their friends played touch football after school. The sheer fun of running free could never be topped. As for May, he found it hard to visualize her as a prim and proper young girl. How could anyone, especially a child like May, not been allowed to run free?

"Never? Not even when you were a little girl?"

A shadow came over her eyes. Her smile dimmed and she shook her head. "In my country a royal is not allowed to be a little girl. And especially not when she is the heir to a throne."

Wade couldn't imagine a precocious child like May being forced to behave as a miniature adult. If he had his way, he would take her in hand and show her how to make up for her lost childhood. Unfortunately, time was running out, and, worse luck, her future wasn't up to him.

But there was still today.

Wade rescued her Frisbee, gave it back to May and fought the temptation to dust the grass off her slacks. "Go ahead. Be yourself," he said. "Just don't run too fast."

How fast was too fast? May wondered as she trudged barefoot back to the starting line. With less than two days to convince Wade she wanted him to make love to her, she knew she had to move fast whether Wade liked it or not.

For that matter, she wondered, how far was too far? And how fast was too fast? One thing she was sure of—that five minutes of being held in Wade's arms hadn't been as far as she wanted to go.

Chapter Eight

"We're in luck," Charlie crowed as she ran across the grass. She waved a colorful flyer being distributed throughout the park. "The Band with no Name is putting on a concert in the park's amphitheater tonight!" She smiled happily at May. "We're all invited to stay for dancing."

May glanced down at her bare midriff and shrugged helplessly. As if all that exposed skin wasn't bad enough, there were her grass-stained slacks and bare feet to consider. Participating in a Frisbee throwing contest dressed like this was one thing, but dancing in public was something else. She looked so bedraggled her own father wouldn't have recognized her. She wanted to stay to dance, but she had to live with her conscience, and the rules of proper behavior had been drummed into her ever since she'd learned to speak. "I would like to, but not like looking this," she said regretfully. "I look terrible."

Wade followed May's woeful gaze to her bare midriff, blinked and swallowed his opinion of how wonderful he thought she looked. As far as he was concerned, the more disheveled May became, the more intriguing he found her. And the more intriguing he found her, the more he wanted to hold her in his arms and kiss every delectable inch of her.

His mind's eye flashed back to the first time he'd noticed May. A vision in her sheer, white cocktail dress, white satin pumps, every inch of her regal bearing spoke of her royal lineage. In spite of the invitation in her eyes as she'd glanced at him over the rim of her glass of champagne, she'd been clearly untouchable.

Even with the change in her, she didn't look touchable.

It was strange how May had actually managed to become a young woman he might have known back home in Nebraska. Not only in the way she looked, but in her determination to have fun before life's responsibilities caught up with her.

Still, knowing that the change in May had to be temporary, he didn't know whether to be happy or sad for her. Deep in his heart he realized that who-ever she appeared to be on the surface today wasn't all that kept them apart. The fact was that the flesh-

and-blood woman beneath the carefree surface was still Dowager Duchess Mary Louise of Lorrania and he was her bodyguard.

He steeled himself to remember that…for both their sakes.

In spite of Mike and Sam's obvious uneasiness at the carefree way May ran barefoot and laughing through the grass, the last thing he wanted to do was to take that happy smile off her face. If listening to a small, four-man band in the park was what May would like to do tonight, he wasn't going to stop her.

As for actually dancing under a star-filled moonlight sky with May in his arms, that was another story. He couldn't imagine a thing he needed less or wanted more.

"Hey, guys," Charlie called when she finally collapsed on a bench. "I'm starving. How about the rest of you?" She gestured to the fast-food restaurants that lined the street across the park. "Name it. Dinner is only yards away."

Dan, on the losing side of the contest with Wade, and obviously grateful he hadn't been the one to call it quits, muttered an Amen."

"I am hungry, too." May rubbed her waist longingly. "I would like to try some different American food tonight. I noticed an interesting place across the street. Chinese?"

"Sure." Wade collected his Frisbee and ambled up to the bench. He was hungry, too, but his hunger was more of a soul-satisfying kind. His real hunger was for her. Knowing it was an impossible dream, Chinese would have to do.

He watched May tally up the scores. This afternoon she resembled a bright, joyful young woman enchanted with the new world in which she'd found herself. A world light-years removed from the royal palace in the never-never fairyland of Baronovia. A country that time had finally caught up with. Unfortunately, Baronovia was a small country located in the turbulent heart of Europe. And the United States had finally taken notice of its strategic location.

In another time and in another place, he would have found a way to share her world. Instead, fate had decreed that he had to protect her from herself and, not too coincidentally, from him.

He tore his eyes away from the small grass stain on May's upturned nose. Covertly admiring her while she chased Frisbees didn't cut it for him. And, now that the Frisbee-throwing contest was over, touching her was definitely a no-no. He put his hands in his pockets before he did the unthinkable and reached to wipe the stain away.

"Dan and I'll go across the street and order," he said briskly. "You and Charlie can look for a quiet

spot for a picnic.'' As he spoke, a school bus full
of children pulled up a few yards away. ''And, for
goodness sakes, stay away from the Frisbee-throwing area.''

''I would like to choose what I eat,'' May ob-
jected over the shouts of fifty eager preteens scram-
bling out of the bus as if they'd been let out of a
cage.

He remembered her food-shopping binge at the
Old Post Office with a groan. If he let her choose,
there wouldn't be anything left for anyone else.
''Don't worry, we'll bring back a little of every-
thing,'' he assured her as he dodged a Frisbee.
''You're better off remaining somewhere Charlie,
Mike and Sam can keep an eye on you.''

At the reminder she might still be in danger, the
look in May's eyes turned bleak. He was sorry to
dampen her enthusiasm, but after her near abduc-
tion, he wasn't prepared to give an inch. Her safety
was number one on his list and that included having
Mike and Sam present. As far as he was concerned,
the more distance he put between May and himself,
the better off they'd be. He motioned to Dan, and
they took off at double time across the grass dodging
Frisbees.

Obviously resigned to a picnic, Mike ambled off
to the car. When he returned, he carried a blanket.
''Okay, where do you want it?''

"How about right there?" Charlie pointed to a secluded spot under a tree at the edge of the park where a water fountain glistened in the sun. "You guys must be prepared for everything," she said admiringly.

"Yeah," Mike answered as he spread the blanket for the picnic. "Got a first-aid kit in the trunk, too, not that I expect to have to use it." He paused for effect and gazed grimly at Charlie. The tone of his voice was more of a threat than a question, but he knew that the unthinkable had happened. He was attracted to the one woman whose personality was light-years different from his. A woman to whom security was a dirty word.

Straight-faced, Charlie raised her right hand. "You don't have to worry about me. I'm cool. Besides, what could be dangerous about a picnic dinner in a park and a band concert afterward?"

Mike looked over at May. "And you, Your Grace?"

She raised an eyebrow. When Mike didn't back off, she added in her regal voice, "I am cool, too." She heard Charlie giggle in the background.

"Then we agree, Your Grace. No surprises. But I want to make something clear." Mike took a deep breath. "I want you to tell me if you see anyone who remotely resembles your father's bodyguard. Or any other member of your father's entourage."

May nodded.

Mike took a stand at one edge of the blanket. He didn't look convinced. She wasn't surprised. After all, she had dodged him and his partner for two days.

While they waited for Wade and Dan to come back with dinner, Charlie stretched out on the blanket, pillowed her head on her arms and studied May. "In the mood for some frank girl talk? Or am I supposed to remember who you are?"

"Not at all." May dropped down beside her and rubbed a sore toe. "It would be a relief to be treated normally. Most people are too afraid to tell me what they think. All they are able to see is my title."

Charlie laughed. "I'd never be able to function as a concierge at the Blair House if I let anyone's title intimidate me. So, as long as you're sure you don't mind, here goes. It looks to me as if Wade is very interested in you."

A hesitant smile curved May's lips. "How can you tell?"

"Simple. He looks at you as if he'd like to take a bite out of you. But he knows he can't. Why else would he invite me and Dan to tag along with you guys today?"

Surprised, May gazed thoughtfully at the fast-food shop across the street before she looked back at Charlie. "That means he likes me? I would have thought he would prefer to be alone with me."

Charlie laughed and lowered her voice. "I guess you don't know American men very well. Take it from me, they all like to believe there's safety in numbers. As long as Dan and I are around he thinks he's safe."

Before May could reply, a Frisbee sailed over the grass, grazed her forehead and fell in her lap. A trail of blood started to trickle down her cheek. To her dismay, Sam and Mike rushed to stand in front of her, hands on their open jackets, guns at ready. Shocked, she saw Mike grab the Frisbee and throw it into the nearby fountain.

Time stood still as the two boys who had thrown the Frisbee skidded to a stop in front of them.

"Are you okay, Your Grace?" Mike finally checked her over while Sam headed for the trunk of the car. Seconds later, he came rushing back with the first-aid kit.

"You are overreacting, gentlemen," May answered tightly, her lips set in a grim line. "It's just a scratch. There is no need to frighten the children." She motioned to Mike to retrieve the Frisbee and throw it to the two boys.

"No, ma'am," Mike answered as the boys scrambled back to the other children. "Precautionary measures. It could have been a bomb."

"A bomb?" May's blood ran cold at the reminder she was still in danger. And that the happy afternoon with its carefree laughter wasn't real. Any more real than May Baron. She wiped the blood off her face with a piece of gauze Sam handed her. "Surely you are mistaken? This is a public park, filled with children."

"All the easier to get to you, Your Grace." Mike handed her a bandage to put on her forehead. He straightened his jacket and motioned Sam back to stand at the rear of the blanket. "From what I understand, you're not safe as long as you're in D.C. As for what might happen when you get home…" His voice trailed off, but the implication was clear. She was in danger, and so were they.

At Mike's dire prediction, May's happiness vanished. The sheer joy of running barefoot in the grass gave way to reality. She shook her head and sank back down on the blanket beside Charlie.

"No wonder Wade doesn't want to have anything to do with me," she said. "He's afraid of what could happen."

"That's not true," Charlie said sympathetically. She patted May on the shoulder. "Wade isn't afraid for himself, or he wouldn't be in the navy. I'm sure he really cares for you. He's just afraid of complications."

"What good is it if Wade does care for me? Or if I care for him?" May asked bitterly. "He is right.

There is not only no future for us together, I am a danger to him as long as he is with me.''

Charlie pressed May's hand to comfort her. ''That's not the complications I'm talking about. I can't pretend to know how it feels to be a woman in your position, but what I do sense is that you care for him as much as he cares for you. Right?''

''For all the good it will do me, yes.''

''Then all I can say is that it's too bad you have to leave D.C. so soon, or I'd tell you to go for your heart's desire.''

May started to confess she *had* intended to go for her heart's desire, to make love with Wade. But that was before the Frisbee accident reminded her of the futility of her falling in love with an American naval officer. Or, with her current identity, living peacefully in the United States. With or without him.

Wade and Dan finally returned. Wade carried a large cardboard box; Dan carried a tray of cold drinks.

Wade eyed the quiet quartet. For a woman who had just won a Frisbee throwing contest, May was much too quiet. Beside her, Charlie looked glum. Mike's and Sam's body language didn't look any better.

At the sight of a small bandage on May's forehead, an electric shock of apprehension ran through him. He dropped the box on the blanket. "Something happen here?"

"Nothing we couldn't handle." Mike said over his shoulder as he continued to survey the grassy area surrounding the blanket. "But it sure proves I was right. We don't belong here out in the open." He glanced worriedly at Charlie.

"For Pete's sakes," Charlie cut in. "You guys act as if someone had gotten killed." She knelt and reached for the cardboard box. "All that happened was that some kid threw a Frisbee and it inadvertently hit May in passing." She glared at Mike. "These guys reacted as if someone threw a bomb at her, and they frightened half of the kids in the park."

Wade felt the blood drain from his face. He dropped to his knees in front of May and searched her face for more injuries. "Are you sure you're all right, May?"

She dismissed him with a slight smile. "It was only a Frisbee that some child threw to his friend and missed. I hardly felt it brush my forehead."

"Are you sure?" He felt a cold lump in his gut at the thought of what might have happened if the Frisbee had actually been a bomb. If anything had happened to her on his watch he would never forgive himself. He started to reach for her, then remembered they had an audience.

"I am sure," she answered with that dismissive gesture he'd come to know so well. A gesture he sensed was designed to hide her emotions. She looked away and searched through the box filled with closed cartons. "How can I tell what to choose?"

Wade swallowed his questions. Any questions and answers would have to come later, but the possibilities of what could have happened to May tore at his insides.

If only he could tell May how important she had become to him without giving himself away.

At the same time he realized Mike and Sam were right. He'd foolishly given in to May's pleading to have a normal evening, but she was too vulnerable to life-threatening danger to dismiss the incident lightly. From now on he vowed to stick to May like glue.

"Why don't we try to forget what happened. After all, it was just an accident," Charlie said. With a warning glance at Wade and Mike, she handed May a cold drink. "Don't forget the fortune cookies. You never know. It might tell you you're about to win the lottery."

"Fortune cookies?" May turned away from Wade's concerned gaze. She took a cookie, broke it open and silently stared in disbelief. "You will soon receive your heart's desire."

A sharp pain crossed her heart. If ever there was a prediction she longed to believe, it was this one. Impossible, but precious to her. She tucked the slip of paper into her shirt.

"My fortune says I'm going to take a long trip soon," Charlie said with a laugh. "I wish. What does your fortune say, May?"

May shrugged. "It doesn't matter. It is only a game." With a message she longed to believe.

"You have such wonderful things to eat here in your country." May told Wade as if she wanted to change the subject. "I shall have to ask my father to consider inviting American fast-food companies to Baronovia."

If he didn't already know that dot-on-the-map Baronovia was the land that time forgot, Wade would have thought she was putting him on. No fast-food franchises? Impossible.

"May," he said, relieved at the change in the atmosphere and wide-eyed at the mental picture of golden arches among the wooded countryside of the Baronovia that May had described. "American foods are from around the world. They were brought here by immigrants."

To his secret pleasure, May nodded thoughtfully. "That is good," she answered in that old-fashioned and precise way of speaking that tickled him so. "I shall speak to your trade mission representative when I return home. Perhaps we can have them brought to Baronovia, too.''

"Don't tell me you're personally acquainted with members of our trade mission?''

"Of course,'' she said in a pragmatic voice. ''As the heir to the throne, I was trained in all aspects of government. Including trade with other countries.''

A closed look came over Wade's face. May instantly realized she had made a mistake in reminding him of her royal status—a status that stood between them. But maybe not forever, she thought as she recalled her earlier intentions to experience love before it was too late. There was still one night left to her to make her dream come true. She thought back to Charlie's ''girl's talk.'' If what her new friend had said was true, Wade did care for her. If so, and if she intended to fulfill her dream, learning the meaning of love would have to happen tonight. And in no other man's arms but Wade's. For after tonight there would be no private moments for them. Perhaps not even to say goodbye.

She couldn't tell Charlie of her intention. No matter what the future held for her, fulfilling her heart's desire would have to remain a secret—a secret she would have to hold close to her heart forever.

"Thank you, guys, that was great,'' Charlie said when the remains of the picnic were cleared away.

"Come on, May. Let's go over to the amphitheater before all the good seats are taken."

Wade glanced at the wary expression on Mike's and Sam's faces. Like them, he'd been hoping Charlie would forget about going to the concert, let alone any dancing. "Are you sure you want go over there? The night's turned cool."

"No problem," May said with a shy smile at Mike. "I am sure Mike will let me borrow his blanket if I am too cold."

"You would be wiser to go on back to the Blair House, Your Grace," Mike answered. "No use exposing yourself to danger if you don't need to."

"I need to," May said firmly. "Tonight is the last night I can be myself. Tomorrow night there is the ball. Wade?"

Wade's gaze locked with May's. Instinct told him the Secret Service agent was right, but his heart urged him to allow her this one last wish to be herself. It was the last thing he could do for her. Besides, if dancing under a moonlit sky was a legitimate way to get to hold her in his arms, he didn't intend to say no. "We'll go for a while," he replied. "If it gets too cold, we can leave."

The night was getting cooler, but Wade's body warmed at the thought of dancing under a starlit sky with May. He gathered the Frisbees, her sandals, the blanket Mike handed him and held out his hand to

May. Tonight was going to be a night they would both remember.

The amphitheater was almost full when they arrived. The musicians were warming up. A park official was patrolling the crowd and asking everyone to be seated. Over Mike's protestations, they had to split up for available seats. Wade was paired off with May, and the unhappy agents were two rows behind them. Dan and Charlie sat across the aisle.

Wade reminded himself that while May had obviously started out pretending to be attracted to him, somewhere along the way her charade had become real. No way could she look at him with such longing in her eyes when she thought he wasn't looking if she didn't truly care for him.

He tried to remember she was foreign royalty, here for a state visit. To remember to treat the remainder of May's stay as a duty, no more, no less. A duty he hadn't asked for that had wound up changing his life.

Tomorrow night when the clock struck twelve at the grand farewell ball being planned by the State Department, May Baron, the woman he'd fallen in love with would turn into the untouchable Dowager Duchess of Lorrania.

And he would go back to being a pragmatic lawyer in the Judge Advocate General Corp, U.S.N. A man who hadn't fallen in love before now. A man who had wound up giving away his heart to a woman who would fly out of his life in two more days.

The more he thought of never seeing May again, the more he ached to ignore the rules of behavior that had been set out for them. He wanted to take her back to his loft apartment and show her how precious she'd become to him.

He heard Mike's voice admonishing him to keep cool, calm and collected as long as he had May with him. He had to remember how close May had come to danger in spite of, and maybe because of, his efforts to take care of her. If the kidnapping had happened in Baronovia, he probably would have been beheaded by now.

Wade's heart ached at the empty future May had told him she faced when she returned home to fulfill her duty. A duty that called her home—a life she'd described as a gilded prison.

If there was going to be any precious memories created for May to take home with her, the next move would have to be up to him.

Chapter Nine

As if they were diamonds scattered by an unseen hand across the dark-blue velvet sky, stars glittered down at the park. Colorful lanterns hung from the trees surrounding the small amphitheater swayed in the evening breeze. On the bandstand, the band switched to the internationally known popular song from the movie *Titanic*, "My Heart Will Go On."

If ever a night had been made for dancing, Wade mused as he took in the enchanted settings this one had to be it.

The small area in front of the bandstand set aside for dancers quickly filled. Without missing a step, the overflow moved to the surrounding grassy area.

Wade thought fast. If dancing was the only legitimate way he could take May in his arms without Mike sending him dark, warning looks, he'd do it. At least it would give him time to think of a plan to be alone with May later.

He glanced at May sitting silently beside him, mouthing the lyrics to the song. Her expression spoke a thousand words.

"May?" he said, and reached for her hand. She turned around to gaze at him. At the longing look he saw in her eyes he rose and held out his arms. "Care to dance?"

With a glance at Mike, May hesitated. Since the earlier Frisbee accident, she couldn't ignore his warning about the danger of being in an open and unprotected area. And yet, now more than ever, she wanted Wade's strong arms around her. To hold her, to give her one more precious memory to take home with her.

Praying the gods were with her, and convinced no one could possibly recognize her the way she looked tonight in slacks and Wade's oversize white shirt, desire threatened to overcome caution.

In the end it was Wade's grim expression when he had exchanged words with Mike on the subject of protecting her that convinced her. Anyone determined to harm her would have to go through him. She would be safe with Wade.

What mattered most to her was that, if this was to be her one last chance to be held in Wade's arms, to have his lips brush her forehead, his low, full voice whisper in her ear, she would take it.

With the knowledge that the night had to end

soon, she smiled up at Wade. "Yes, please. Just for the few moments before I have to leave." Her luminous eyes spoke for her.

Held in Wade's arms, May felt as if she had drifted into a fairyland. A fairyland where diamonds shone in the skies instead of stars. Where soft, green grass became a dance floor. And where the scent of summer flowers filled her senses.

The park had turned into a fairyland where she'd found her Prince Charming.

She smiled as she leaned into Wade's warm and muscular chest. Washington, D.C., the capital of the most powerful country in the world was an odd place to think of as a fairyland. How could she have guessed a state visit accompanying her father to a country thousands of miles away from home would turn her life into a fairy tale come true? Or that she would find herself dancing barefoot on a summer's night in a park where grass tickled her toes. And where the strains of a song about lovers separated by circumstances they couldn't control would break her heart. The words hit too close to home.

Stranger still was the only man who could have turned into her Prince Charming, Commander Wade Stevens of the United States Navy.

It had been his eye-catching masculine figure in his pristine naval uniform that had first caught her interest. An interest that had been fueled by his smile and the frank look of admiration on his face when their eyes had first met.

She had decided then Wade was a man who could be easily manipulated, but time had proved her wrong. Strong and dedicated to a duty he hadn't asked for, he had turned out to be a man's man when he had to be, a woman's man when he cared to be. And, at the moment, she thought with a pleased smile, her man.

She gazed up at Wade and nestled closer to him. His lithe body fitted hers as if it had been molded to her. His arms held her with a gentle strength as if he never wanted to let her go. Warmed by the strong beat of his heart, his warm breath against her forehead, she became more aware of the growing sexual tension between them. At the same time she realized that, while she had been attracted to Wade from the first time she'd seen him, she hadn't counted on falling in love.

She ached to be one with him tonight, each a half of a whole person. To taste the love that had been denied to her in the past. And to forget she was Mary Louise and that there was a tomorrow.

If only time *could* stand still.

"Wade," she murmured when the thumping of her heart reminded her they would soon have to part. "Perhaps I should leave now."

Wade gathered his wayward thoughts, tightened

his arms around her and brushed her upturned lips
with his. He couldn't help himself. "You called?"

"I said perhaps it is time for me to go back to
the Blair House."

"Soon, but not just yet," he said with a glance
at the ever-attentive Mike, frowning from a few
yards away. "After all, we might have to pack a
lifetime of conversation into the next few hours."

"It is true. Time is rushing by so quickly," she
said wistfully. "Do we really have hours?"

Wade glanced at the giant clock on the church
spire across the street. "One or two," he said, trying
to keep the regret from his voice.

Suddenly the band swung into what was obviously its forte—the music from *Dirty Dancing*.
Cheers went up and the crowd went wild.

When the press of dancers pushed him closer to
May, Wade drew in a sharp breath. His nerve end-
ings tingled with desire, and a hot, sensual pounding
heat throbbed through his loins. Every touch of her
soft body sent a wave of desire through him.

If his superiors, or, heaven forbid, May's father,
the prince, could see them now, sure as heck his
career would be over. Somehow he didn't care. It
was too late. His career wasn't important. Not when
he'd already lost his heart.

If only he hadn't kissed her.

Duty and honor told him he should call a halt to

the dancing and take May back to the Blair House before she realized just what "dirty dancing" entailed. He had started to explain when the startled look in her eyes changed to pleased surprise. To his delight she glanced around her and began to mimic the other dancers. Left in the middle of the dancers, he had no choice but to follow.

"You actually like this?" he asked the next time her derriere bumped his.

She gyrated around him, and raised her arms above her head and wiggled. To his dismay, the shirt she'd tied under her breasts moved higher and exposed more skin. "I had no idea what I was missing," she laughed as they passed each other.

Wade got a strong feeling that once May returned home, Baronovia would never be the same.

And neither would he.

When the band changed to a more sedate popular song, he held her so close he could feel the rapid beat of her heart. He nuzzled the hollow of her neck, inhaled her sweet scent. Dirty dancing had been fun, but holding her in his arms was more to his liking. "I can't think of a better way to spend time together. How about you?"

She shook her head. A smile came over her face, a bounce came back into her step. "Tell me about Wade Stevens."

Wade was startled. "Why?"

"I would have liked to know you as a young boy," she replied as she ran her fingers through the hair at his nape. "As it is…"

The reminder these were possibly the last few private hours they would have together and she wanted to take some memories with her tore at Wade's heart. If she'd asked, he would have told her about his own fortune-cookie prediction. And that he had made a wish for a lifetime of conversations with her. A lifetime of making love to her in a place where there were no tomorrows.

What was more relevant, was the hot, sensual, pounding beat of his heart that throbbed through him.

"There's not too much to know about me other than what I've already told you," he said wryly. "As a boy, I thought farm life was boring and, like a lot of country kids, wanted excitement."

"And have the past few days with me been exciting enough for you?"

He winced as his slacks grew tight. "Yep." Especially the dirty dancing. "Although I could have done without the rotten tomatoes. That was a first time for me."

"Me, too. For that I apologize again."

"No apology necessary. It comes with the territory," he answered, and held her more closely.

"Have you always wanted to be a lawyer?"

"No. I actually dreamed of going to sea. When I finished high school I persuaded the town mayor to have our local congressman put my name up for Annapolis. Soon after, my interest turned to the law. Since grad school, instead of finding myself on a ship, I've been stationed mostly here in Washington."

May listened thoughtfully. Her love had had to work hard for everything he wanted. All she'd had to do was to have been born to a life of luxury and privilege she didn't want. "I am sorry I involved you in all of this."

"Don't be sorry—I'm not." He risked a kiss on her forehead. "Knowing you has taught me something. I already knew how to look beyond the surface, but now I know to recognize what's real and what isn't."

"And am I real?" May asked wistfully.

"You bet!" he answered. "Why?"

Her eyes were troubled as she gazed up at him. "Because at times like this I am not sure just who I am. Mary Louise of Lorrania or just May."

He outlined her lips with a gentle forefinger. In the background the band began to play "Good Night, Ladies," the traditional music that marked the end of an evening of dancing.

"You're real, all right, sweetheart. Don't let anyone tell you you're not. You'll always be May to me. Tomorrow night is time enough for the duchess to reappear. And, just in case I've forgotten to tell you," he went on as he brushed her cheek with his lips, "I realize how much I needed someone like you in my life."

"Then it is a pity that tomorrow must come too soon."

Wade saw a mist come into her eyes. The haunting look of love cracked the shield he'd tried to weave around his heart to protect himself from their parting.

Torn between wanting May the way a man wants the woman he loves and knowing any lasting relationship between them was impossible, he threw caution to the wind. He wanted her and he wasn't going to let the evening end without showing her how much.

He ran his fingers through her hair, caressed her nape. Tonight was special, and May was too special to let the night end now. He'd never felt this way before. From the look in May's eyes, neither had she.

"Come home with me tonight, May," he whispered. "Come home with me and let me love you. Let me love you even if tonight is the only time I will be able to."

"How did you know that you were my heart's desire?" she whispered back, her eyes alight. "How did you know I wanted to make love with you to-night?''

"Easy," he murmured. "You saved the message in your fortune cookie."

She gazed at him suspiciously. "How did you know what the message said?"

"I picked it up when you dropped it a few moments ago. I figured you kept it for a reason. As if that didn't clinch the deal," he said with a killer grin that captured her heart all over again, "there's that invitation in your eyes." He couldn't bring himself to tell her his own factory-produced fortune cookie had said the same thing.

"Oh, no!" May hid her face hidden in his chest. "Do you think everyone knows?"

"Don't worry, sweetheart," Wade assured her. "It's enough that I know."

May gazed up at him, love shining in her eyes. "I would like to go with you," she said with a sob in her voice, "but what about Mike and Sam? They watch my every move. And Charlie and Dan?"

Wade glanced over at the Secret Service agents. Standing in the semidarkness that surrounded the dancers, the men presented a formidable problem. But there was a possible solution.

Too conservative to be considered an exciting escort by May, Mike had obviously been interesting enough to capture Charlie's interest. He could tell she was smitten by the way she kept arguing with Mike to get his attention. As for how Mike felt about her, there was no overt interest, but Wade knew better. Mike was a goner.

Charlie was the one he could depend on to help him!

As for ditching his friend, he intended to make sure Dan knew his presence was no longer required. No sweat.

"Pretend to shiver, sweetheart," he said in an undertone. "I'll tell Mike you're cold and I'm taking you home. You do know how to pretend, don't you?"

She smiled wryly. "I have been pretending for one reason or another most of my life," she whispered as she started to shiver. "This is easy."

He wanted to kiss every inch of her. Not because she was good at playacting, but because she was obviously as eager for the next step in their relationship as he was. "Good, then that's settled. I'll tell Mike we're stopping at my apartment to get the rest of your clothes."

Rocked by sensual emotions she could scarcely understand, May still hesitated. As much as she loved Wade, she didn't have to be told that the longer they were together, the more danger he might find himself in.

The responsibility bred in her from birth told her

she should thank Wade for the garish Wal-Mart sweatshirt she would always connect with him. She should thank him for escorting her during her stay in D.C. and go home with the Secret Service men. And, most of all, she should remember she had to go back to living the life she was born to.

She would never stop loving Wade. She would never forget the manly side of him that had drawn her to him at first glance or the uniform he wore that made him appear dangerous.

She would never forget his military bearing—the way he managed to make her feel safe even in the midst of danger. And for the desire that glinted in his eyes and echoed in her when he turned his gaze on her.

She should let him go, she knew. More for his sake than for hers. The only problem was she loved him too much to let the night end this way. She yearned to have it end in his arms.

"Are you sure you want to do that? You might get into trouble."

"Sweetheart, if I'm not mistaken, I'm already in trouble up to my eyeballs." Wade glanced at the ever-watchful Mike, but with the warmth of May's body burning against his, he no longer cared about the consequences. "I've probably broken every rule in the Secret Service manual on how to be a bodyguard. So, let me do the worrying for both of us."

Mike looked doubtful when Wade explained that May was cold and that after a quick stop at his loft apartment to get May's belongings they were going back to the Blair House.

"Only if Sam and I drive you there...sir."

The belated formal address spoke volumes. Mike wasn't about to let May out of his sight. Not willingly, anyway.

"Okay," Wade improvised, "you guys can drop us off and we'll catch up with you later."

Mike's "you wish" expression sent goose bumps up Wade's back. He swallowed a protest. Raised to tell the truth, and sworn to honesty by the very nature of his profession, he couldn't insist on sticking with a lie.

The dance music stopped, and the musicians started to pack up their gear. The lanterns dimmed, and the dancers groaned and reluctantly drifted away. Overhead, dark clouds appeared and thunder sounded.

"Something going on here?" Charlie asked as she and Dan joined them.

"Not much," Mike replied and beckoned to Sam. "You might say the party's over. Guess it looks as if we're in for a storm, anyway. We're about to head back to the Blair House."

The thick silence was broken only by the muted

sound of voices and the sound of crickets that filled the summer air.

Charlie exchanged telling glances with May. "I'll take May home in my car," she offered. "You two can drop off Wade and Dan."

Mike snorted. "Yeah, like I can trust you."

Charlie huffed indignantly. "Just what do you mean by that? You act as if I'm one of the bad guys!"

"You're not taking the duchess anywhere—not while I'm around," Mike said. "It was bad enough when you gave the commander's address to the guy who wound up trying to kidnap her."

"He was her father's bodyguard," Charlie sputtered in her defense. "How was I to know he was a Baronovian nationalist who wanted to get rid of her family?" With her fists balled, she looked mad enough to deck Mike.

Dan grabbed her around the waist and held her back. "The man's right," he said. "I'll go with you." With an apologetic look at Wade, he added, "The only way to be sure May is okay is if Mike takes her home himself."

After a few speechless moments, May entered the fray. This time as Duchess Mary Louise. "That will be enough, gentlemen. I will go home the way I came."

Mike nodded his satisfaction and led the way to

the car. To Wade's surprise, as soon as Mike's back was turned, May quietly mouthed the word *later*.

Thwarted and frustrated, Wade trailed May and the two agents back to their car. At Mike's silent gesture, he joined May in the back seat.

Later? Wade's senses stirred at the question. How much later? And where?

He eyed his silent companion and kept his next question to himself.

What did May mean by "later" anyway? Evading the Secret Service was obviously one of May's talents. As to how she intended to accomplish her reappearance at his apartment, that was another. In either case he wasn't about to ask. Not when he had the gut feeling that what he didn't know couldn't come back to bite him.

After being dropped off at his apartment, he strode the floor impatiently, trying to find the answer to his questions.

Two endless hours later, tired of pacing his loft apartment and worrying himself sick over what kind of fool stunt May might have come up with next, he heard a brisk knock on the door.

May?

He glanced at his watch, let out his breath and headed for the door. After two near misses with danger behind her, surely she knew better than to tempt fate by showing up at his apartment. What he *had* expected was a telephone call asking him to meet her at the Blair House.

Even that idea had seemed shaky at best, but at least she wouldn't have been roaming around D.C. in the dead of night.

He peered through the peephole in the door, swore silently and took a second, quick-appraising look.

He opened the door and stared.

"May?"

Chapter Ten

A heartbeat later Wade recognized his visitor. May's impish grin gave her away. To his dismay, she was alone.

May proudly returned his incredulous gaze. "This is a good disguise, yes?"

"A good disguise, no!" Wade managed, his eyes roaming May's figure. Admiration for her chutzpah filled him, but he didn't intend to say anything that would encourage her. Somehow or other, he had to get it through to her that her life could be at stake. "Is this your idea of 'later'?" he asked ominously.

Her smile faded; she took a cautious step backward. "You *did* expect to see me tonight?"

"Yes, but..." He was so rocked by the sight of May's unusual appearance he wasn't sure exactly what he had expected to happen tonight.

After May had flirted with danger for the past three days, he sure as hell hadn't expected her to dodge her bodyguards tonight. Let alone cross D.C. and show up at his apartment at midnight.

He hadn't counted on her looking like this, either.

"I thought we agreed you weren't going to go anywhere without Mike and Sam," he growled. He checked the hall again, just to be sure she was alone, pulled her into the apartment and locked the door behind her. "How did you manage to get here without someone knowing it was you?"

She smiled mischievously and motioned to her outfit. "Because I look like this. And because I used the servant's entrance at the Blair House."

His heart pounding with his anxiety, Wade took a longer look at what May clearly regarded as a disguise. Her dress was a gray, very snug linen uniform that covered her from her throat down to mid-calf. The original owner of the uniform had to have been built like a stick, for unlike the chambermaid May was made up to resemble, the dress was snug enough on her to show her pert breasts and her delectable derriere. An item Wade carefully noted.

A white lace collar buttoned at her neck, and cuffs were at her wrists. To further make a charade of the disguise, her hair had been tinted red and was covered by a stiff white cap.

His gaze wandered down. Her legs were sheathed in serviceable gray cotton hose that didn't come close to hiding their exquisite shape. A prim white apron and sturdy black shoes completed the disguise. One thing was clear, Wade mused uneasily, no chambermaid had ever looked as sexy as this. Someone *must* have noticed her.

Her appearance was so different from the first time he'd noticed her he had to bite his tongue to keep from laughing. Never mind the other outfits she kept turning up in.

He went on to check out her makeup. She'd painted her lips a bright red, dark-brown mascara and eye shadow almost obscured her eyes. Thank God, he thought as he smothered a groan, her delectable cheeks had escaped her attention. They glowed like ripe apricots.

She looked like a different woman. Anyone who'd known the old one would never have recognized her.

Except him. He would know her anywhere.

Wade took a deep breath and concentrated on mentally counting to twenty. It was either calm himself now or say something he might regret.

"How did you get here?" he finally managed. The possibilities at this time of night made him blanch.

"Taxi cabs seem to run twenty-four hours a day in your country," she reported happily.

"A taxi? Thank God you didn't take the underground," he growled. "Don't you realize half of the

Baronovia malcontents currently in D.C. could have followed you here?'' The idea that she had been able to evade her Secret Service bodyguards and had caught a taxi undetected blew his mind.

Just thinking of what could possibly have happened to May, alone and defenseless in D.C. at midnight, left him shaken. "Maybe a stunt like taking a cab would be okay in a small country like Baronovia," he went on, "but it sure isn't okay here in D.C."

She looked dubious. "In the middle of the night? And with my disguise?"

Ah, that disguise. He'd better not say anything about it. Because if he did, he wouldn't be able to stop looking or wanting to touch her in all the places that she, in her naiveté, thought were covered.

He didn't know whether to kiss her or shake her until the pearl earrings she wore in her delicately shaped ears fell off. He settled for taking her in his arms.

"Wade?" she said cautiously, "Is something wrong?"

"Ask me later." He sank down on the couch with her in his lap. "Right now let me hold you until my heartbeat returns to normal, if ever. As a matter of fact," he added as he buried his lips in the soft velvet of her throat, "it hasn't beat normally from the first time I set eyes on you."

Her look of satisfaction almost undid him.

Determined to make her pay for worrying the day-lights out of him, he gathered her more closely in his arms. With a groan of despair, and realizing he'd probably already lost the argument, he kissed her forehead, the corner of her eyes and the elusive dimple in her right cheek. When she kissed him back, the how, when and where she'd escaped her body-guards didn't seem to matter anymore. It was enough she was here.

He was more in love with her than ever. Even more so now than when she'd thrown herself into the spirit of dirty dancing in the park and almost rocked him off his feet. A spirit so abandoned she'd drawn an audience. And Mike's disapproval.

"Do you have any idea of what you do to me?" he asked when his heart finally resumed its normal beat. "Even in that outfit you're wearing?"

"Charlie borrowed it from one of the chamber-maids at the Blair House," she laughed. "We thought the uniform would make a perfect disguise. I promised to return it in the morning."

Charlie? Wade gave up. The trail to finding May had become a little more convoluted with the Blair House concierge in the picture. He no longer had any doubts of the eventual outcome of May's flight. Once she was discovered missing, the logical trail would lead the Secret Service agents here.

He'd hoped the feisty and innovative Charlie would have read his mind and come up with an idea to get May and him together tonight. He just hadn't expected Charlie to go so far as aiding and abetting May in her escape. Certainly not after her last run-in with Mike over disclosing his home address to the prince's treacherous bodyguard. Sending May across town in the dead of night was the last idea he'd expected Charlie to come up with.

In the back of his mind, he remembered Under-secretary Logan's threat: if anything happened to May there would be hell to pay. Wade shuddered. With May here in his arms, he couldn't afford to dwell on it.

The ticking of the kitchen clock reminded him time was running out. No matter what might happen later, he thought as he hugged May closely, she was here now.

"We have the rest of the night before someone realizes you're gone, sweetheart," he said while he still had the will to take her home if that was what she wanted. "Are you sure you know what you're doing?"

She turned her face to his with a look that sent his body stirring and his senses crying for relief. "I am sure," she said quietly. "No matter how many hours we have together, they will always be mine to remember."

She took off the starched cap that covered her hair and threw it aside.

Although he couldn't bring himself to make the first move, this was the invitation Wade had been waiting for. But not before he could be sure May understood what he intended. And not before she realized their relationship couldn't last beyond tonight.

To Wade's delight, May reached for him. In a heartbeat he drew her close and kissed her. "You'll never be sorry," he whispered into her lips.

One by one he took out the pins that held her hair away from her face and ran his fingers through her silken tresses. "Tonight is precious to me, too," he murmured, "If I had my way, tonight would go on forever."

"We can pretend it will. And that tomorrow never has to come," she said with a smile on her lips and in her eyes.

"Let's try." He unbuttoned the lace collar at her throat and slowly, teasing her, teasing himself, he undid the buttons on the dress. Once he had drawn it off her, he stroked the soft, glowing skin of her shoulders, kissed the velvet skin, the soft curve of her breasts and looked questioningly into her eyes. "If you're sure…"

"I am sure," she said softly, and put her arms

around his neck. "I have never been more sure of anything in my life."

Wade gathered May in his arms, slipped off the rest of her clothing and strode to the alcove that housed his bedroom. Before he lowered her to the bed, he paused to kiss her deeply, making her his.

"Your turn," she said, eyeing his clothing with an appraising look.

"Got it." He grinned and began to take off the rest of his clothing.

"Not without me," May said softly. She wanted to help him, to feel his skin slide across hers. She wanted to hold him until she could feel his heart beating against her sensitive breasts.

She reached for his shirt, her fingers stumbling at the unaccustomed task, unbuttoned it. Ran the palms of her hands across his bare, muscular chest. She gently kissed the vein that throbbed at his neck, then slid the shirt down off his shoulders.

Her hands lingered at his lithe middle, stroked the taut muscles that jumped at her touch. This was the only time in her life she had known sexual foreplay, let alone initiated it. Or touched a bare man with her eyes open and with an invitation trembling on her lips.

Every nerve ending in her body cried for the sexual relief she had heard whispered about but had never experienced.

"Wade," she murmured into his bare, salty shoulder, "I have to tell you something before we go any further."

"Now?"

"Yes," she cried, even as his fingers delved into private places. Even as bursts of sensation ran through her.

Wade brought his face up until his lips touched hers. "Changed your mind?"

"I'm not sure," she said with a shaky laugh. "What I want to tell you may sound strange. Maybe it is you who will change your mind."

Wade smothered a sigh and pulled back. He leaned over her and ran a forefinger around an are ola of one nipple. "Shhh, sweetheart. There's no need to talk. I already know."

She was trying to tell him something he'd already guessed. May was as close to being a virgin as a woman could be who had once been a wife.

"I must," May said. A tear pooled at the corner of her eyes. "I must tell you, so that you understand why I am different from the women of your country." When she was sure she had his reluctant attention, she went on. "At home we live as we have lived for the past hundreds of years. It is almost as if Baronovia is not part of the twenty-first century."

A wry smile covered Wade's face as he toyed with her other nipple. "Maybe you've been luckier than you know. Anyway, I have a feeling things are going to change.''

She waved away his comment. ''Marriages in my family have usually been for convenience. As was mine.'' She averted her eyes and twisted a corner of the blanket as she spoke. ''What I am trying to tell you is that although I was married for two years, I was never loved. Our marriage was largely to beget an heir. My husband was never a real husband. I never felt I was a real wife. I thought it was my fault, until I found out he had a mistress to whom he had given his heart. By the time we married, he had no heart left to give me.''

''If the memory hurts so much, don't think about it.'' Wade pulled her into his arms and soothed her brow with his lips. ''That was yesterday, this is now.''

''It is not something easily forgotten,'' she said with a wistful expression, ''but it is something I felt you had to know.''

Wade longed to erase the frown that crinkled her brow, to put a smile back on her face. To show her what a real woman she was.

One thing for sure, his May had to be one gutsy woman to have lived with such archaic traditions. And to be able to turn into the strong and determined woman she was today.

He held her hands to his lips and, lingering to

savor each moment, kissed her fingers one by one. "That part of your life is over. Just think about to-night."

"Show me," she whispered as she nestled closer into his arms.

"Let me love you, sweetheart," he murmured into the side of her throat. "Let me show you the passion you have buried within you."

There had been a time when giving herself to a lover would never have entered May's mind. Taught from birth to accept responsibility, and often reminded she was the heir apparent to the throne, she had never questioned her destiny. She realized now that she had lived as a puppet.

Until she had met Wade and had fallen in love.

Attracted to Wade, and without realizing what she might be doing, she had planned to sleep with him. For once in her life she had wanted to know how it would feel to be a real woman. She had wanted to sleep with him without being in love.

She knew now she had only fooled herself. To her delight, she found herself in love for the first time in her life. Just as she had no doubt from the tender way Wade gazed at her that he loved her back.

But would it be fair to him to have made him fall in love with her only to lose her in the end?

And, once they had made love, would she be able to walk away without breaking his heart—and hers?

She couldn't bear to think about that.

Wade rummaged in the drawer of the nightstand for a foil-wrapped package before he finally bent over her and stroked her neck. "Sweetheart," he murmured with a tender look that hit her like a bolt of lightning, "you think too much. Just let yourself go, and feel."

He was right. She couldn't let the night go by without learning the pleasures of making love. For surely the marital interchanges between her and her late husband hadn't been love at all. Tears of joy filled her eyes as Wade kissed her fingers, then trailed a line of moist, warm kisses from her wrists to her elbows, to her shoulders and down to her breasts, leaving bursts of pleasure behind.

Her fingers roamed over his back as she drowned in the sensation of the heat of his mouth, his lips brushing her eager breasts. Lost in the magic of being skin to skin, of his body that fitted her as if he had been made for her, she wanted Wade with every breath of her body, every beat of her heart.

In his arms every dream she hadn't dared to dream had come true. Surely, their coming together had been more than sex. It had been a man and a woman in love giving of themselves to each other.

THE CLOCK STRUCK FOUR. Wade eased out of bed and stood gazing down at his beloved May. With the summer storm still raging outside, he planned to get her back to the Blair House before she was missed.

Until she murmured in her sleep. "I love you, Wade."

His heart turned over, his pulse raced. She loved him! He'd already decided May was no longer playing a game, but he hadn't counted on her actually falling in love with him.

He'd been right about her. Under her disciplined surface she had been loving and passionate. Even wanton. If tonight had been a fantasy never to be repeated, he intended to make it last. What difference would another hour make? he asked himself. What was another hour when it might be the last few private moments they would have together? After all, he'd fallen deeply in love with her, too.

He told her so, not sure that she'd heard him. Telling her he loved her was his parting gift to her. A gift to ease her soul when she remembered how she had given herself to him.

"Wake up, sleepyhead." He tickled her under her chin. "It's almost time for Cinderella to return to her palace."

"Not now, please." A sleepy smile curved at the corner of her lips. Her exotic green eyes flirted with him before they closed and she started to drift back to sleep. "Maybe later."

Wade had to smile at her childlike comment. He knew better. With dawn just around the corner, there would be no more "later" for them. He pulled the blankets off the bed and tickled a bare toe. "Nope. Now."

May blushed and tried to cover her nude body with the only item remaining—a pillow. It was one thing to make love with Wade in the dark shadows that filled the small corner of the alcove. It was quite another to have the man she had loved throughout the night standing there gazing at her with knowing eyes.

Unfortunately, he was right. She slid to the edge of the bed and looked around for her dress. "All right, but I have to shower and wash the color tint out of my hair."

He looked at her speculatively. Maybe he wasn't going to take her right home after all.

Ignoring the blush she was certain covered her from head to toe, she let him pull her to her feet and led her to the small bathroom. "Sounds good. Come with me."

In the bathroom she snatched a fresh towel from a pile on a shelf and watched with interest while Wade turned on and tested the water. Until Wade asked her, "How hot do you want it?"

Her mind flashing on the night's sexual play, May managed to shrug. She might have been a novice of the game a few hours ago, but she sensed there was still more to learn about loving. Her senses responded to what could be an invitation to further passion. Duchess or not, she was more than willing to take it. She wanted to make love one more time. To have something to remember him by.

He stepped into the shower and held out his hand. Captured by his unwavering look, she dropped the towel and joined him.

Lukewarm water splashed over them as Wade slowly ran his lathered hands over her body, cupped her tingling breasts. He nibbled on her earlobes, her shoulders, ran his hands over her hips and down her legs.

"Do you want me to stop?"

Wordlessly she shook her head. There might not be a tomorrow for them, but there was still tonight. And although she hadn't acknowledged it, she'd heard his vow of love. The knowledge that he loved her, too, warmed her heart.

Achingly aware of his breath on her skin and his desire for her, she took the soap out of his hands. "My turn," she said. Only this time he had no clothing to take off. But then, neither did she. Smiling, he handed her the soap. She started at his chin, where a faint shadow of beard rasped against her hands. She moved down over his broad shoulders, his chest, to his narrow waist. She hesitated and looked up at him with a question in her eyes.

He laughed. "Later," he said, a promise in his voice. He reached behind her to turn off the water.

"My hair," she gasped. "I still have to wash my hair."

He parted the shower curtain and reached for a plastic bottle of shampoo. "Let me," he said. He rubbed the shampoo into his hands and carefully and massaged her wet and tangled hair. His hands slid over her scalp, her neck, slowly and sensually until she shuddered with renewed longing. "Wade," she begged. "Enough."

He grinned down at her and shook his head. "Not yet." He lathered his hands with soap, ran his hands over her hips and down her legs. Stroke by stroke, he rekindled the fires that had burned within her all night and, to her astonishment, took her to heights she'd never dreamed possible.

"I want to touch you again, too," she repeated, and ran her hands over his back, reveling in the flow of his muscles under her probing fingers. She slid her hands around his waist and met his seeking lips. "I never guessed it could be like this," she began. "I never—"

He stopped her with a another deep kiss. "You

don't have to guess anymore, May," he said as he kissed her breasts. "Not anymore."

She protested when he held her in his arms and took deep breaths. She loved everything about him, wanted everything he could give her, to remember in the empty days ahead. She grasped his shoulders, wondering why he had stopped, afraid to speak lest she break the magic that surrounded them. "What?"

"Could I interest you in going back to bed?" he murmured. "I don't think you've been loved the way you deserve to be loved."

"I have no complaints," she said, smiling up at him through the stream of water that flowed over her like a warm summer rain. "What else could there possibly be?"

He stopped and reached over her shoulder to turn off the water. He felt as if he were drowning in her eyes. "I'd like to show you how much I love you before you leave."

"I love you, too," she whispered. The air in the shower was filled with electricity. The woodsy scent of his shampoo filled the steamy room. His strong, masculine chest and chiseled thighs sent waves of renewed longing through May.

"There's more."

She pressed against him. "Show me."

With a chuckle, Wade picked her up in his arms and swung her up in the air. Had it only been three days ago that they'd met? she wondered as she looked down into his smiling eyes. How could she have lost her heart to him in so short a time?

His lips on hers, Wade took her back to bed and explored every inch of her as if he wanted to imprint her body in his mind. Moments later, skin to skin, heart to heart, May felt as if she'd dived headlong into an ocean wave. A wave that curled and spiraled to great heights before it peaked and came crashing down over her.

How would she be able to say goodbye to the man she'd fallen in love with? May wondered as ecstasy faded and every inch of her continued to tingle. How could she go back to the life her father had planned for her without Wade? How could she go back to pretending to be a woman who wasn't her at all?

Beside her Wade stirred and glanced at the clock. Time had gone by so quickly he hadn't realized dawn was about to break. Taking May home now wasn't going to be as simple a matter as he'd thought it would be. "We have to leave, May. I want to take you home while it's still dark."

She scrambled out of bed and started to dress. Each piece of clothing she put on that would take her back to being the duchess threatened to bring tears to her eyes. Even though it broke her heart, she knew Wade was right. It was time to return to reality. "I'll take a taxi."

"No, sweetheart. I'm taking you home."

She paused for a moment, then shook her head. "No! You must not. What if someone sees you? There will be trouble!"

He threw on a shirt, jeans and bent to find his shoes. "It's you I'm worried about, sweetheart," he said as he straightened and took her in his arms for one last kiss. "As for trouble, I'll take my chances."

Chapter Eleven

Undersecretary Logan shook a sheaf of papers under Wade's nose. "Dammit! I warned you, Commander! I warned you to take care of the duchess, to see to it she was safe. Against my better judgment I even gave you inside information about the imminent signing of a high-level agreement between ourselves and Baronovia so you would realize the importance of your assignment!"

Furious, Logan paced behind his desk, and glared at Wade. "I know I stressed the importance of keeping the lady happy, but, God knows, I didn't think you'd be stupid enough to give away the store. I tried to help you accomplish what I thought would be a simple and enjoyable task—a man escorting a pretty woman around D.C.!" He paused to take a deep breath. "So what in the hell could have been more simple than that?"

"Yes, sir. I mean, nothing, sir," Summoned to

the State Department an hour ago, Wade stood at attention. The air-conditioning in the office added to the chill in Logan's voice. Beneath his immaculate summer-white uniform a fine sheen of sweat covered him.

Wade's mind whirled with the worst scenario he could have thought of. He'd been the front and center player in dozens of court appearances, but he'd never felt as uncomfortable as he did now. But then, matters had never been this personal. The official papers crushed in Logan's hand were obviously Secret Service daily reports on the duchess's recent escapades. Knowing what had to be in the papers, Wade bit his lower lip. Did Logan know May had returned to Wade's apartment and had spent the night there?

Playing hide-and-seek with irate Baronovian nationals to keep May safe had been bad enough. The ominous tone in Logan's voice spoke of worse to come.

He wasn't worried about himself, it was May's possible encounter with her father he worried about.

Logan shook the papers under Wade's nose again. If he'd been any angrier, smoke would have poured out of his ears. "I trusted you, Commander! I trusted you so completely I didn't take the time to check the daily reports on the duchess until this morning. And what did I find?"

Wade knew the answer as well as Logan did. The duchess had escaped her bodyguards, not once but three times. She'd had rotten vegetables thrown at her by disenchanted Baronovian nationalists. And, last but not least, she'd almost gotten herself kidnapped. Forget dancing in the park.

Logan might be upset by the events he'd read about in the reports, but May hadn't been, Wade thought fondly. She'd taken it all in stride. As far as he was concerned, she was a steel magnolia if he'd ever met one.

Even if trying to keep a single-minded woman like May safe hadn't exactly been a piece of cake, at least he'd tried. As for making her happy, well, that was another story, he thought as he swallowed hard. He'd keep those thoughts to himself.

Logan threw the papers on the desk and slammed into his seat. "The prince wasn't very happy to hear about all of this, I can tell you. Damn near chewed my ear off this morning. And as for you, Commander," he said crisply as he glared at Wade, "it was only the duchess's intervention that kept him from demanding your head."

Wade's heart raced as he faced Logan stoically. If May had intervened and Logan was still angry, maybe the worst was yet to come.

"Oh, what's the use," Logan growled at Wade's silence. "The lady is taken with you, although why,

God knows. You've been a hell of an excuse for a bodyguard.''

Wade gazed front and center. The way the undersecretary was looking at him, the remark was no compliment. But at least Logan hadn't said he was aware May had spent most of last night with him. Or that Logan knew he'd dropped May at the service entrance to the Blair House just as dawn broke through the muggy darkness. They'd been lucky— cleaning crews were in the process of changing shifts. No one had questioned her in her uniform when she'd covertly mingled with the new crew. Although he'd noticed a D.C. policeman winking at her as she passed. So much for tight security.

Wade cleared his throat when Logan stopped to take a deep breath. ''About tonight, sir…''

Logan frowned. ''What about tonight?''

''The farewell ball. I was to escort May—'' He froze at the look that came over Logan's face. Damn!

''May?'' Logan repeated ominously. ''I assume you're speaking of the duchess?''

''Yes, sir, I am.'' Wade went on to explain that in order to appear as ''normal'' tourists, he and May had decided to call each other by their first names in public. And that she'd gone on to assume various ''disguises'' so that no one would recognize her. As if, in any shape or form May's appearance or behavior was normal, he thought fondly. She would have stood out in a crowd no matter what he called her or, for that matter, what she wore.

Logan eyed Wade in disbelief. "After tonight, Commander, the matter is out of my hands, thank God. As for you, take it up with the prince. He's asked to see you. At the Blair House. Now!"

Wade cleared his throat. "Sir, about tonight…"

"What about tonight?" Logan growled.

"The farewell ball, sir. I just told you I was to be the duchess's escort."

Logan eyed him with distaste and waved him off. "Forget it, Commander. We don't want to see you within ten feet of the duchess. And that's an order."

WADE'S FATE was waiting for him at the Blair House. On his way in, he spotted Charlie, the fly-by-the-seat-of-her-pants concierge trying to look as if she'd faded into the woodwork. Mike Wheeler, the agent assigned to the Blair House guests lounged at the foot of the staircase leading to the guest rooms upstairs.

Wade glanced toward the balcony landing at the top of the stairs in time to see May standing there. When he nodded reassuringly, she gazed at him for a moment, then turned and disappeared. Wade sensed he was in deeper trouble than he'd thought.

He had expected May to reappear when he was

ushered into a private study, but thank God the prince was alone.

"You asked to see me, sir?" Wade said when Prince Alexis's aide closed the door behind him.

The prince motioned to the leather armchair positioned in front of a highly polished Louis XV desk. Decorated in tones of wine and gray, the room seemed to reflect the somber look on the prince's face. Not good.

"Yes." The prince regarded him thoughtfully. "First, I feel I must thank you for keeping my daughter from harm during her outing in your city. She has suggested she was to blame for insisting on visiting places she knew would not be acceptable. In fact," he added dryly, "my daughter speaks highly of you."

Wade swallowed hard at the compliment. He had a premonition this wasn't the end of the matter.

The prince went on. "I would speak of the unfortunate lapse of judgment on the part of Serge, my former bodyguard."

The steel in the man's voice made Wade wonder if the bodyguard had already met the fate he'd so richly deserved or if he would have to wait until the prince returned home.

"In view of our respective countries' new relationship," the prince continued, "it was and is important that my daughter become acquainted with your country and its people. The trip to the museum was fine, as perhaps was the Old Post Office. I am told, however—'' he stopped and frowned ''—there was no Secret Service in attendance at either of those two places. My daughter has explained the lack of Secret Service bodyguards was her idea.''

Mike Wheeler's report. What else had the agent told the prince?

Wade's heart sank even further when Prince Alexis fixed his steel-gray eyes on him.

''However, allowing Mary Louise to dance barefoot in Georgetown Park after an attempted kidnapping seems to have been an error of judgment on *your* part, Commander. What were you thinking of to have allowed this?''

Unfortunately, Wade knew exactly what he'd been thinking of when he'd allowed May to get the better of his good judgment—teasing green eyes, full and tempting lips and most of all, May's indomitable spirit. Falling in love with her had come later.

''I was trying to keep her happy during her stay here, sir,'' he replied. ''I thought normal activities would be the ticket to the real Washington, D.C.''

''Normal, you say?'' Prince Alexis's eyes sparked, but Wade sensed he wasn't amused. ''That is an interesting choice of words.''

''Yes, sir.'' Wade swallowed hard.

The prince steepled his hands and regarded him

over raised eyebrows. "As a military man, and especially as a bodyguard, surely you realize the safety of your charge was more important than her so-called happiness."

"Yes, sir. No excuse, sir." For May's sake, Wade couldn't tell her father how she had yearned to be free of royal restraints. How she had begged to be free, if only for a few days. Pleading he was a lawyer and not a professional bodyguard was immaterial. He'd been given an order by his superiors. May's exotic sex appeal or not, he should have insisted they visit every stone monument in D.C. for every minute of her stay. And given her the lessons on the history of the United States her father had hoped for.

God willing, Wade prayed mentally, no one would know exactly the lessons he *had* taught May. Or that in the process he'd learned a lot about himself.

He'd been so involved in his naval career he hadn't taken the time to stop to sample life's fringe benefits. He'd helped investigate, defend or prosecute dozens of men and women he hadn't known and had never see again. What he hadn't done was to find a woman who cared for him or children to give his life meaning.

In another life May could have been that woman.

It didn't seem fair that he had found the woman he couldn't have.

As soon as this assignment was over, he intended to ask for a leave, camp on a deserted island long enough to get over loving and losing the woman he'd first come to admire and then to love.

The prince's voice caught his attention. "You should know, Commander, that while my infant son is now my heir, the duchess is still second in line to the throne of Baronovia. As such, I cannot allow her to become involved with someone outside the royal family. And, especially someone who is not from my country."

Wade felt himself flush. He sensed May had shared more of what had gone on between them during the past three days with her father than museums and dancing barefoot in a park. Obviously, not where she'd spent last night, thank the Lord, but obviously, enough for her father to comprehend she and Wade had strong feelings for each other.

He felt like a fool. He'd read enough about European history to realize May's importance to the Baron dynasty hadn't ended when her half brother had been born. He should have remembered her place in history. A place that had no room for a farm boy from Nebraska.

"However," the prince sighed, "what is done is done. I have spoken to the duchess and she has agreed not to see you again." He stood and regarded Wade with a firm but compassionate look. "I assume you are ready to give me your word that you will honor her commitment."

Duty, honor, country. He should have known it was no different for Duchess Mary Louise of Lorrania than it was for him. His throat choked with emotion, Wade had no choice but to nod his agreement.

"Good." The prince rose and held out his hand for Wade to shake. "Again, for what you tried to do for my daughter, I thank you. And, Commander," he added when Wade saluted and started to turn away, "my daughter thanks you, too."

Wade blindly made his way out of the study. He might have been taken off escort duty, but he'd hoped at least to see May one last time tonight at the ball. He had to tell her he loved her. He had to tell her he would remember their few days together for the rest of his life.

If only he could have been allowed to say goodbye.

MAY ENTERED the reception room where members of the U.S. State Department, Congress and various foreign ambassadors and dignitaries had gathered for farewell courtesy calls prior to the gala ball scheduled for tonight. The room had been decorated with the flags of the U.S. and Baronovia. Waiters wearing white gloves were moving among the guests, passing trays filled with champagne flutes and hors d'oeuvres. A chamber music quartet played quietly in the background.

She was dressed in a pale-green linen suit, a pearl necklace was around her neck and pearl earrings were in her ears. Back to her royal persona, her lustrous hair was gathered in a chignon at the base of her slender neck. To the casual observer she appeared to be every inch the Dowager Duchess of Lorrania.

Or so, Mike Wheeler, the duchess's personal bodyguard, now that the Commander had been relieved of the duty, thought at first glance. But since he'd spent the better part of the last two days with the duchess and her JAG escort/bodyguard, he knew better. He sensed that behind that cool, royal facade there was a broken heart.

This wasn't the woman who had enjoyed eating an ice-cream sundae in a neighborhood ice-cream parlor like an ordinary tourist. A woman who had happily licked the spoon clean when she was through and had eyed the commander's banana split with interest.

This certainly wasn't the same woman who had shocked him out of his shoes by engaging in dirty dancing under a moonlit sky.

Nor was she the woman who had gone on to dance the evening away barefoot in Georgetown Park in Wade Stevens's arms.

Mike was willing to admit he was a dyed-in-the-wool, go-by-the-book Secret Service agent. But he was still human enough to feel a pang of pity for the sad-eyed woman who stood beside her father exchanging polite conversation with guests.

Whatever troubled her, he was damn sure it had to do with the JAG commander, Wade Stevens.

He shook his head. Give him a working, democratic country anytime. A country where men and women were created equal. Where men and women who loved each other were able to marry. And where inherited titles didn't mean a damn.

Of course, Mike had a strong doubt that someone like the duchess would ever have had a chance to fall in love with the commander if Charlie Norris, the Blair House concierge, hadn't stuck her nose where it shouldn't have been.

He scowled at Charlie, now unobtrusively making her way around the room to ensure the waiters were doing their job properly. How in the hell had that woman been hired by the State Department for such a responsible position when she was such a blithe spirit? Irresponsible, was more like it.

Across the room May steeled herself to respond politely as each of the guests was introduced to her father and then to her. The women were dressed in colors of the rainbow, the men in dark blue or black business suits. A few wore uniforms. But none, in her opinion, could hold a candle to Wade Stevens. The man she'd loved and lost in the space of a few short days.

His attraction hadn't been only for the way he looked in his gold-trimmed white uniform, she told herself as she smiled and acknowledged another introduction. Wade had been a man's man, strong, fearless and as dedicated to duty as she was.

She thought of his masculine, tall, lean body. Of the eyes that shone with laughter and love. And the strong arms and long, muscular legs that had gathered her to him and given her memories to cherish for a lifetime.

Most of all, she thought with an ache, Wade had shown her there could be love in the act of making love. And in doing so, had chased away her memories of empty days and lonely nights.

"May?" her father whispered when they were momentarily alone. "Are you going to be all right?"

May gazed into her father's concerned eyes. He, too, must have known times in his life when duty came before his personal desires and lived through it. As his daughter, she could do nothing less. "Thank you, Papa. I am."

"Your Highness," Logan's voice broke in. "I

would like to present Congressman Holt of the Sovereign State of Virginia and Mrs. Holt.''

With a nod the prince turned away. May took a deep breath and tried to look happy. Under her studied smile, her heart ached until she felt it would surely break in two.

After learning the meaning of love in Wade Stevens's arms, how could she return home to a second loveless marriage?

DESERT ISLANDS were definitely out. Wade muttered to himself as he strode the street near the Blair House in jeans and the white shirt a member of the Baronovian delegation had returned this morning.

What he *did* intend to do was to stay far enough away from May to keep his promise, but close enough to make sure she was safe. If he was faced with an attitude adjustment, he intended to do it right here in D.C.

He glanced down at the shirt. Wearing it had been a big mistake. All he could think of was the way May had looked in it tied high above her waist with her midriff showing.

The streets around the Blair House were clogged with long, black limousines ferrying visitors to an afternoon reception at the House. A house where the late President Truman had resided while the White House had been renovated.

Wade's thoughts drifted to the festive farewell ball taking place later tonight.

He wondered how May would look. In another couturier gown that revealed how exquisitely she was made? Of all the outfits May had worn and discarded, it was the Wal-Mart sweatshirt that lingered most in his mind. And the woman who had worn it.

The sound of laughter coming from Donovan's Pub drew him like a magnet. The scent of beer wafting through the swinging doors was an invitation to forget. He'd never been particularly fond of liquor, but now seemed a good time to have a few beers.

He found a seat at the end of the counter. The bartender wandered up and wiped the already spotless counter in front of Wade. "What'll you have, me boy?"

While Wade tried to collect his thoughts, the man smiled. "Troubles, is it? Here, have a Guinness. It's a sure cure for what ails you." He reached under the counter, opened the green bottle and put it in front of Wade.

This had to be Donovan himself, Wade thought as he nodded his thanks. To his limited experience, it was only the Irish who had the ability to read a person's mind, to be so open about it and so ready to offer sympathy.

"Now, don't tell me 'tis women trouble you're

havin'," the man said as he put a small dish of pretzels in front of Wade. "Not a fine boyo like yourself. In the military, are you?"

Wade had to smile. "How did you guess?"

"You have that air about you, did you know? It's the way you sit, so strong and sure." He leaned over the counter and nodded wisely. "Take it from a man who knows, whatever is bothering you is temporary. I'd stake my pub on it."

Wade paused in the act of taking a swallow of the tart-smelling beer. "How can you be so sure?"

Donovan winked. "Wait and see," he said, and moved away to serve another customer.

Wade took a long swallow of Guinness, then another. And another until the bottle was empty. Without a word, Donovan sent a fresh bottle sliding down the counter toward him.

Wade carefully chose a pretzel to go with the beer and regarded the new bottle. To drink or not to drink? So far, his mind was clear—too clear. Voices from the small table at the end of the counter filtered through to him.

"How would you like to take a few days off, Mr. Johnson? A paid vacation, you might say."

"When?" The voice sounded surprised but eager.

"Starting tonight."

"Can't, dammit! I'm working the Intercontinental tonight. Some big shindig—a prince is giving a ball.

Every member of the service staff has been called to duty.''

"Then they won't miss you, will they?'' the first voice coaxed.

Wade swung around and covertly gazed over at the table. The only ball he knew of going on tonight was the one Prince Alexis of Baronovia was giving. The ball where he would have been May's escort—if he hadn't made the mistake of falling in love with her.

Why was a member of the Intercontinental service staff being asked to take a hike?

"Tell you what,'' the older, dark-haired man went on. "You can take that vacation. I'll take your place.''

The man called Johnson stared at him. "Why would you want to do that?''

His companion waved airily. "I've always wanted to see how the other half lives.'' He reached into his pocket, took out his wallet and put two fifty-dollar bills on the table. "How's this for starters?''

While Wade watched, dumbfounded, the man added another fifty. "Well?''

Johnson reached for the money. "You got it. How long do you want me to be gone?''

"Just for tonight,'' the man answered. He put his wallet back in his pocket. "Now, how about your uniform?''

"It's just the same old black pants, black tie and white shirt," Johnson answered. "They give you a special cummerbund that matches the decor when you report for duty. No big deal."

To Wade's surprise, the two shook hands and left separately.

Wade sat speechless, possibilities running through his head. Why would someone pay to serve at a ball?

Visions of the protest group in front of the Blair House the other day swam into his mental view. A picture of the hulking dark figure that had followed them in the National Portrait Gallery followed. The numbers added up when May's attempted kidnapping completed the picture.

Whatever the dark-haired man wanted, it wasn't something good. And from the slight accent in the man's voice, he could well be another disenchanted Baronovian national.

Heaven only knew what the man had planned!

Wade reached for his cell phone and started to dial Undersecretary Logan's office, then realized that Logan was undoubtedly at the Blair House this moment.

Wade searched his photographic memory, dialed the number for the Blair House, identified himself and asked to speak to Logan. A few minutes later a polite voice informed him Logan was too busy to take his call.

Wade wasn't going to give up. If Logan was out of the picture, he asked to speak to Mike Wheeler.

"This had better be good," Mike's voice said over the phone. It sounded as cool as a blast of winter air.

"Not good but vital," Wade answered. "I overheard a conversation that sounds as if something's going to happen at tonight's ball. I want to be there tonight to prevent it and I want your help."

"Nice try, Commander," Wheeler answered. "But take it from me, nothing is going to get you into that ballroom tonight. The word is out."

"Hold on!" Wade hurried to tell the agent what he'd just overheard. "From what I just heard, I'd stake my life that Serge wasn't the only player in May's attempted kidnapping. There's something else going on, and it's going to happen tonight. I feel it in my bones."

"If something is going on, our intelligence would have heard about it," Mike replied. "So far everything looks normal. The prince and his entourage are leaving in the morning, so relax."

"Come on, Mike," Wade pleaded. "Just let me be there tonight to make sure May doesn't get hurt!"

"Good try, but the answer is still no," Mike replied. "I know how you feel, Commander, but I have my orders, and they're to see to it that you don't get anywhere near the duchess." There was a pause before Mike added in an undertone, "if it will make you feel any better, I intend to stick close to her tonight, myself."

Wade swore into the cell phone. Someone had to listen to him! He tried again, only to hear a dial tone. Seething, he beckoned to Donovan and handed him a ten-dollar bill. "Keep the change."

Donovan beamed. "You look better already, me boy," he said with a broad grin as he pocketed the bill. "The Guinness does it every time. Now, don't take no for an answer."

Wade paused long enough to shake Donovan's hand. "Thanks, I don't intend to."

Chapter Twelve

For the first time in his career as a U.S. naval officer, Wade intended to disobey orders. Even if it meant risking his career.

The conversation in Donovan's bar had sent chills up and down his spine and left him no choice. He might have agreed not to try to see May, but he sure as hell hadn't agreed to stop thinking about her while she was still in the country.

Come hell or high water, he mused as he cut across a busy street, he intended to do whatever it took to keep the woman he'd loved and lost in the space of a few short days safe from harm. If it got him busted in the process, so be it. At least he'd be able to live with himself.

He didn't have to be joined hip to hip with May in order to watch over her. To make sure she wasn't the target, he decided, all he had to do was to be where he could keep an eye on May and on the surrounding territory.

He glanced around him. There had to be some way to get inside the Willard Intercontinental ballroom without being noticed. Maybe he could wear a disguise so that no one would recognize him. Whatever it took would be okay with him. As he'd assured Donovan, the genial bartender, he wasn't going to give up without a fight. He'd meant it.

Wade strode home, burning up the pavement in his frustration. Scenario after scenario on how to crash the ball without getting thrown out on his ear or starting a riot whirled through his mind.

He was back in his apartment surveying the contents of his closet for possibilities when a mental lightbulb turned on.

All he had to do was to go as himself.

AS IT TURNED OUT, getting into the hotel ballroom for the start of the ball turned out to be a snap. It had just been a matter of taking a cue from the way May had managed to come back to the Blair House early that morning without being recognized. Wade waited for the next crowd of guests to arrive and slipped in behind them.

By nine o'clock he found a place off to the side of the entrance to the ballroom where he could observe the action. Considering the nature of the celebration, a treaty between the United States and Baronovia, attendance was brisk. Tuxedoed United States Secret Service personnel politely checked each guest as they arrived.

After a few minutes spent observing the drill, Wade recognized that the crush of new arrivals was often too great for the agents to take more than a cursory look at ID.

Ten minutes later a large group of guests arrived, laughing and talking up a storm. After noting they were largely uniformed military men and women, he made up his mind. This group was his ticket inside.

All he had to do was to murmur "JAG" as if he were part of the noisy group and move on before he was questioned. His white naval dress uniform with its short tuxedo jacket, gold stripes and the bright yellow cummerbund around his waist would do the rest.

With his heart in his throat, he joined the crush at the door as if he belonged with them. Luck was with him. In the confusion of handling so many people, he was waved on.

Once inside the ballroom, he took a flute of champagne offered by a passing waiter. He checked the man's uniform to see if it was the same as described by the man at Donovan's. Sure enough he wore a white shirt, black trousers, green tie and a bright-green cummerbund. To Wade's disgust there so many dark-haired waiters dressed identically moving among the guests that he didn't have a prayer of recognizing his prey.

The celebration tonight was like no other diplomatic ball he'd ever seen. Opulence was evident everywhere; in the decorations and on the attendees. There had to be a ton of gold braid and medals on the foreign men's uniforms. The uniformed members of the U.S. armed forces were also dressed to the teeth. Wade hoped he was the only one present who had a Baretta conveniently stuck in the back of his cummerbund.

He found a corner where he could observe the action without being noticed.

The room had been transformed into a fairy-tale ballroom. An undercurrent of excitement filled the air. Red, white and blue flags of the United States and green, gold and white flags of Baronovia hung from the balconies. Exotic floral arrangements decorated each flat surface around the room. Polished crystal chandeliers glittered overhead. The floor-to-ceiling mirrors were hung with garlands of flowers. A tuxedoed orchestra played for the benefit of dancers.

As he wandered carefully around the ballroom, he recognized a hidden entrance near the double doors that hid a banquet room.

To his dismay, some fool had ordered a small platform set up in front of the orchestra. A microphone stood ready for introductions and announcements. It didn't take a genius to realize that the speaker or speakers for the evening would be prime targets, maybe the prince himself.

They might as well have placed a bull's-eye on the microphone. Anyone with a gun could lose himself in the crowd far too easily for Wade's comfort.

He searched the ballroom for security personnel. He had had no trouble recognizing the formally dressed Secret Service agents by the identifying pin in their tuxedo jacket lapels. The hotel had its own security people. It looked as if every branch of the government had sent in personnel. If what Wade suspected was true, they were expecting trouble.

Moving slowly and purposefully throughout the ballroom, Wade looked for Mike Wheeler or Logan. And, at the same time, tried to avoid being seen by anyone he recognized or who might recognize him.

He casually emptied his champagne into a rubber-tree plant. If there was ever a night when he intended to be sober, this was it. Pausing long enough to trade his empty champagne flute with a full one, he strolled to the other side of the room.

And, to his horror, heard another conversation that sent his blood racing.

"Don't say I told you this," a disembodied voice

said confidentially, "but I understand they're signing the agreement between Baronovia and the United States tonight."

"Agreement?"

"Yes. The treaty that will allow the United States to establish an embassy there. Although, to tell the truth," the voice went on, too loudly for Wade's peace of mind, "I hear there are a number of countries bordering Baronovia that aren't too happy about the United States presence there."

Wade swore under his breath, emptied the flute of champagne into a flower arrangement and moved on. That the treaty was going to be signed tonight was news to him, even if it hadn't been a very well-kept secret. His instincts and the chill that was running up and down his spine told him something unpleasant was going to happen sometime tonight. Thinking of the ominous exchange of waiters at Donovan's he was sure of it.

He didn't know if May was aware of the proposed signing. Or what steps had been made to protect her and her father.

All the more reason he had to find May. Now!

MAY STOOD GAZING out the third-story window at the White House across Pennsylvania Avenue. She could see a long line of tourists waiting to visit what travel pamphlets called "the people's house."

Built along classic lines, the White House was far different from the ornate palace in Baronovia she called home. Built in the sixteenth century, the palace was the classic Central-European castle with hundreds of rooms, battlements and even dungeons. The outer walls were decorated with statues of gargoyles that had sent her into a breathless state of terror as a child.

In stark contrast to what she saw across the street, no one had visited the palace unless invited. And that hadn't been often. Her only playmates had been selected cousins or children of the housekeeping staff. As befit an heir to the throne, even her play had been monitored.

She hadn't made any lasting male friendships during her teen years, either. When the time had come for her to marry, her father had chosen an older, distant cousin for her husband. Both for his lineage and, supposedly, his maturity. To add to her lasting unhappiness, no one had questioned whether or not the man had loved her or if she had loved him.

Her husband's death, although it had saddened her, had set her free. In mourning for the past year, she had led a circumspect life, except for the few days here in D.C.

Until Commander Wade Stevens came into her life.

She leaned her forehead against the windowpane

and closed her eyes, the better to picture again the man with whom she had fallen in love. Wade was tall and handsome in his white uniform with three broad gold stripes on his sleeves. His uniform and his twinkling blue eyes, sandy-brown hair and his memorable smile had drawn more than her attention. So much so that in a short space of time she had tasted love for the first time. With a man who had looked beneath the surface of the duchess Mary Louise and found May. Three days later, just the memory of being in Wade's arms was able to set her on fire.

Taking Wade as a lover had brought her joy and bittersweet memories she would remember for the rest of her life.

"I've pressed your gown, Your Grace. Is there anything else I can do for you?"

"That will be all, Betty," May said to the Blair House chambermaid who had stayed to freshen up the gown May would wear tonight to the ball. "I will dress myself later. Thank you."

When the door closed behind the maid, May realized that by going down memory lane she had been trying to postpone the inevitable: the farewell ball that would mark the end of her visit to the United States. And the end of the love affair with Wade that had ended too soon.

She paced the bedroom and pondered the meeting

with her father this morning. From the look in his eyes she realized he'd guessed, or at least suspected, she had spent the night with Wade. Otherwise why would he have told her she must never see Wade again?

She thought about the distressed look on Wade's face after he'd been summoned to the Blair House this morning and had glanced up at the balcony to see her standing there.

She'd yearned to run down the stairs, rush into his arms and tell him she loved him with every ounce of her being, with every part of her soul. To tell him she would love him forever.

But there had been the watchful Mike Wheeler standing guard at the foot of the staircase. To save Wade from being arrested or, at best, thrown out of the Blair House, she had turned on her heel and disappeared into her suite. She would never forget the devastated look on his face when, for his sake, she'd turned away.

To add to her anguish, there was the farewell ball already underway. A night where she would have to act the role she had been born into, no matter how broken her heart. Another night when she wished she could have been her real self, May Baron. And where all the world would have known Wade was the man to whom she had given her heart.

She gazed at the pale-green silk slip dress lying

on the satin bedspread. At the long, sheer green stole edged with ostrich feathers meant to wear around her shoulders. And at the diamond and emerald tiara that she, as Duchess Mary Louise, would wear on her hair.

Tears slipped unbidden down her cheeks as she wished with all her heart the dress was Wade's big white shirt and she was back dancing in the moonlight. Or even, she smiled to think about it, the oversize sweatshirt with Washington D.C. painted across the front she'd worn as a disguise. The memories were so vivid and the ache for Wade so strong, she wondered where he was tonight. And if he could possibly know, although she'd turned away from him, how much she actually loved him.

WADE SLOWLY MADE HIS WAY through the crowd looking for the dark-haired waiter. Not just any waiter, he told himself. From his years as a trial lawyer specializing in international law, he'd learned to put a great store in body language. He scanned the room for someone who looked uncomfortable, out of place. As if he were playing a role. A man who was trying too hard to look as if he belonged.

A sudden stir at the back entrance to the ballroom drew his attention. Without taking his eyes off the waiters, he sensed Prince Alexis had come into the

room with his entourage. Because there were no
murmured comments about how beautiful the duchess looked, he knew May had to be missing from
the group.

Good. It gave him time to make his way to the
vicinity of the door. To a spot where he could keep
an eye on her movements when she did show up.

He heard a low curse beside him, but before he
could spot the speaker, the door leading to the hall
opened again to a flurry of activity. Heads craned to
see the newcomer. This time it was his May, walking proudly, every inch the regal duchess. His May
carefully hidden from public view.

The crowd parted to allow her to pass. Wade was
relieved to see Mike trailing her, a hand poised at
her back, eyes searching the perimeter as they
walked. Two other tuxedoed agents followed.

Wade's eyes rested on May. She was dressed in
a pale-green silk dress that left her shoulders bare,
hugged her waist and fell to swirl around her trim
ankles. A diamond and emerald tiara nestled in her
hair, and a matching sheer stole hung low over her
arms. She looked lovely, but never as beautiful as
when she'd danced barefoot in the moonlight in his
arms.

Watching her advance slowly into the room,
Wade felt the ache in his heart. The most stylish and

beautiful woman in the room, she was also the most distant.

The enigmatic expression on her face as she passed damn near broke his heart.

He drew back against the wall. Somewhere beneath all that glitter and ostrich feathers was the woman he loved. The knowledge that she was safe for the moment wasn't enough. Not when he was certain that until he found the renegade posing as a waiter, May's life and her father's were in jeopardy. Perhaps, even if the treaty never got signed. Too bad he hadn't been able to convince Logan of the peril the prince and May faced tonight, he thought grimly. But at least Mike Wheeler had kept his promise to watch over her.

Time was getting short. Now that all the players were present, it had come down to catching a would-be assassin—with the only clue a glimpse of a face and lowered voices in a smoky, dim room. And no idea as to who the man might be.

He certainly couldn't be a member of the prince's entourage again, Wade reasoned. The prince was no dummy. After Serge had been unmasked, surely he had had the rest of his entourage from Baronovia checked out. If not some disgruntled Baronovia nationalist, then someone who had been hired as a local hit man to do the dirty work.

Wade made his way around the perimeter of the

ballroom to the kitchen door. If danger came in the form of a man in a borrowed waiter's uniform, he was sure it had to be coming through there.

What if Wade could get Logan to persuade the prince to put off signing the agreement for now? Fat chance, Wade thought considering Logan wouldn't give him the time of day.

In the meantime, there was another problem: the prince had asked him to stay away from May. And since the prince and May were certain to be standing together before the night was through, it meant staying away from the prince, as well.

Wade didn't care what he'd promised the prince. As far as he was concerned, from the moment he'd overheard the conversation in Donovan's bar about buying the regular hotel waiter's time, he'd had no choice but to try to stop the would-be assassin.

Wade carefully noted waiters carrying empty trays into the kitchen and tried to focus on some mannerism or facial feature of theirs he could remember. He waited until each man came back with a loaded tray. The female attendants weren't suspects. At least for now.

With a calculating look behind him, a waiter went through the swinging doors to the kitchen. Noting the man's expression and his narrowed eyes, Wade's senses jumped to full alert. This was his man. No professional waiter worth his salt would push through swinging doors before he made certain he wouldn't collide with someone coming out.

When the waiter reappeared carrying a tray of hors d'oeuvres, Wade followed him. Strangely enough the waiter ignored reaching hands and headed straight to where May and her father were standing.

Warning bells rang in Wade's mind. Why would the waiter ignore the other guests and head for May when it was his job to serve the fragrant tidbits to anyone who wanted them?

The hors d'oeuvres had to contain poison meant for Prince Alexis and the duchess!

Instead of creating havoc by shouting a warning, Wade elbowed his way through the press of guests. Ignoring cries of outrage and the rapid beating of his heart, he prayed he would get to May in time to warn her.

Too late. He was within arm's reach of the waiter when the man offered the tray to May. To Wade's relief, May shook her head. The waiter said something in a foreign language, but May thanked him politely and waved him off.

The waiter bowed and turned away but not before Wade caught a glimpse of the fury in the man's eyes. And knew, as well as he knew his own name that this man was the would-be assassin and would not stop at trying to poison May. He had to find a way to stop him before it was too late.

Frustrated, Wade realized the only thing left for him to do right now was to let Mike keep watch over May while he found Logan and forced him to listen to him.

Wade made for the staircase at one end of the room. He reasoned that if he stood high enough on the stairs, he could easily spot Logan in the crowd. And when he did, he wouldn't give up until Logan listened to him. Even if he had to wrestle the guy to the floor in the process.

The glint of the crystal chandeliers bounced off a mirror at the base of the staircase and caught Wade's attention. To his horror, he caught a glimpse of the waiter, this time returning to May's side, a gun held close to his side. The expression on his face was frightening. Now that all else had failed, the man had to be on a suicide mission!

Wade bounded down the stairs, shoved the people in his way aside and tackled the waiter. Alarmed voices broke out, a woman screamed, and someone called for the police. His face a mask of rage, the waiter struggled to his feet, slammed his fist into Wade's stomach and spit out words easy to recognize in any language. He was sending Wade to hell.

A red haze distorted Wade's vision. "Maybe,"

he gasped as something snapped inside him. "But not before I see you there first."

Wade staggered, then headed for the bastard with the intent to kill or be killed. If the man was on a suicide mission, there was nothing that would stop him except a well-placed bullet.

The waiter came at him again. Wade grabbed his arm, pulled it across the man's back and grabbed him around the neck until the man began to choke. "Enough?"

The man cursed again. "Never!" he hissed as he twisted viciously and broke Wade's hold. He lunged again. This time Wade threw up his arm and caught the punch on his shoulder. Together they fell to the floor in a jumble of arms and legs.

Calls for the police continued to fill the ballroom. Guests screamed and rushed for the doors. Someone shouted for everyone to stay calm before someone got hurt.

The waiter slipped from Wade's grip and made for the staircase. He bounded up a few steps and turned around, gun in hand. Limping, Wade pushed his way to where May and her father stood, frozen in place.

The assassin took cold and steady aim at Prince Alexis and May. "Long Live Baronovia!" he screamed fanatically.

The man's bravado gave Wade the chance he was

looking for. Skidding to a stop in front of May, he reached behind his back and pulled the revolver from his cummerbund. Taking deliberate aim at the gun in the assassin's hands, he fired.

But not before he felt a bullet slam into his shoulder and another into his leg. The last thing he heard before the ground came up to slap him in the face was the sound of May's terror-stricken voice.

Chapter Thirteen

"So, you had to be a hero, didn't you?"

Smothering a groan at the pain pounding at his shoulder and about to crush his forehead, Wade forced himself to open his eyes. Admiral Jonathon Crowley, the judge advocate general himself, stood at the foot of his bed glaring at him. Undersecretary of the navy Logan hovered anxiously at his side.

The admiral's clipped, cold voice made Wade wince. Wondering if he should salute his commanding officer at a time like this, he tried to straighten up in bed.

"As you were!" Crowley said, motioning him to lay back. "I've heard a lot of crap about what happened last night," the admiral went on, "but I'd like to hear your side of the story."

Wade exchanged a meaningful look with Logan before he turned his gaze back on the admiral.

"Well, sir," he said as he struggled to sit up straight, "you might say stuff just happened."

"Stuff? You call taking matters into your own hands, shooting a suspect, upsetting the State Department, not to mention the entire Washington diplomatic community, stuff?"

Wade swallowed hard. From the expression on the admiral's face, it was beginning to look as if the ten years Wade had devoted to his career at JAG were about to go down the drain, and he along with them. "Yes, sir. That is, no sir. I thought I had no time. I felt I had sufficient reason to act immediately."

Crowley glared back at him. "You *are* aware you should have called for backup instead of going solo, are you not?"

Wade glanced at Logan's wary expression. If he was about to go down, there was no use taking Logan, too. Without him, Wade would never have been able to spend the three most exciting and wonderful days of his life; although, he could have passed on the assassination attempt. "I didn't have the time, sir. After I identified the suspect and noticed his gun, I had to act, and fast."

Crowley considered him thoughtfully. Wade's heart sank even lower. "From what I hear, Commander," the admiral finally said, "it sounds to me as if you made this a personal crusade. And you and I know that that's always a mistake.''

Wade gazed at the admiral stoically.

''A fortunate mistake in this case,'' the admiral added before Wade could open his mouth to object, ''but one I hope you do not attempt to try again.''

At the word *again,* Wade leaned back against the pillows, wincing as the IV needle in his wrist pulled tight against his wrist. With May thousands of miles away by now, it wasn't likely he'd be called upon to rescue her again. ''Yes, sir…I mean, no, sir.''

''When you're back on your feet, you'll have to fill me in on the story behind your heroism,'' Crowley said dryly. ''In the meantime, the stack of cases on your desk is growing.'' He glanced at the nurse who had come into the hospital room carrying a tray with a hypodermic syringe and needle. His mouth relaxed into a wry smile as he turned away and motioned Logan to follow him. ''Enjoy your stay here, Commander. I'm sure I'll see you soon.''

Enjoy his stay!

Wade eyed the needle warily. ''Are you sure you have to do this?'' he asked the smiling but determined nurse. ''I've had so many shots in the last twenty-four hours I'm beginning to feel like a pincushion.''

''It will make you feel better,'' she answered cheerfully, and gestured for Wade to turn over.

Wade groaned, turned on his side and accepted the inevitable. Better! He would have felt a lot better about the whole hospital routine if May had been here holding his hand and smiling her encouragement.

So much for heroism.

"AND SO, MY DAUGHTER, I can see you have at last fallen in love."

Seated across from her father in his private study, May met his eyes and nodded slowly. Her mood echoed the somber air the book-lined walls, wine-colored velvet drapes and carpets of the room she wasn't invited to visit unless her father had something serious on his mind. Sensing he wanted to discuss her brief affair with Wade, she would tell him the truth even if she incurred his displeasure.

"With the brave United States naval commander?"

"Yes, Papa."

"The same young man who saved your life, and perhaps mine as well?"

"The same man, Papa."

"The man I asked that you never see again?"

Her heart broken at having to leave the United States without being able to say goodbye to the man she loved, May tried to hide her anguish with a smile. "His name is Commander Wade Stevens, Papa."

"Yes, I know." He picked up a document that lay on his desk and studied it for a long moment. "I felt you would want to know I have been in touch with the United States State Department regarding the heroic gentleman's progress."

May sat forward eagerly. "He is well?"

"Yes." He studied the document again. "I am told that the commander is doing well and is expected to return to duty shortly."

May felt as if the weight of the world had been removed from her shoulders. At least she now knew Wade was well and out of danger. "Thank you for telling me, Papa."

"I regret we had to leave the country before you had a chance to see the commander again, my dear," her father went on. He rose and walked around the desk and laid a gentle hand on her shoulder. "I would have remained in Washington until I was certain of the outcome of the shooting, but the United States State Department advised against it."

"Yes, Papa." The picture of the shooting at the farewell ball and the turmoil that had ensued still haunted her. She had cradled Wade's unconscious figure in her arms until members of the Secret Service had hustled her away from the scene. Still in shock, and under her father's direction, she had been on their private plane headed to Europe by mid-morning the next day.

"By their request, I signed the treaty between our two countries and ordered our return here immediately to prevent any further problems. Considering the uncertain circumstances here, I did not wish to cause the United States Government any further embarrassment by remaining there."

May silently studied her folded hands while her father went to a cabinet. She heard the sound of glass clinking against glass, the sound and scent of a sweet-smelling liquid being poured. He came back and handed her a brandy snifter.

"Here you are, my dear." He lifted his glass with a smile. "Let us drink to the heroic commander. A man who has shown the world what love can do."

Surprised at the toast, May glanced up at her father. Her heart raced at the compassionate expression she saw in his eyes. "What love can do, Papa?"

The prince sat down at the edge of his desk and nodded. "You need not act surprised that I know the truth, my dear. It is obvious only a very brave man or a man in love would have taken a bullet meant for one of us. I suspect your commander is both."

May shuddered at the memory of Wade lying unconscious on the ballroom floor like a broken doll, his immaculate white uniform covered with his blood. And how heartbroken she had been when she and her father had been spirited away even as she begged Wade not to leave her.

Her father squeezed her shoulder. "So as to why I asked you to meet me here... Now that we are home again, you are undoubtedly wondering about my plans for your future, no?"

"Yes," May answered, grateful that her father was kind enough to take the time to prepare her for the future and her place in it. She steeled herself to once again be reminded of her royal position—second in line to inherit the throne. With her half brother still so young, it was only natural for her father to be concerned about her next marriage.

"When you were the heir apparent to the throne, my dear May," he went on with a comforting smile, "I felt it was my duty to see to it that you married a man who would be worthy of becoming the father of a future ruler of Baronovia." He rolled the brandy in the snifter and took a sip. "In affairs of state, I'm afraid there was a time when I had no choice."

A flicker of hope grew in her breast, then died at the serious expression that came over her father's face. "And now, Papa?"

"And now there is your infant brother, Johan."

May warmed at the mention of her baby brother. With blond hair, sparkling brown eyes and a cherubic grin that displayed two tiny front teeth, he never failed to catch at her heart. Not even when he reminded her of the child of her own she had longed for in vain during her own loveless marriage.

"Yes," she said softly. "And now there is darling little Johan, bless his heart. Are you saying you no longer need me, Papa?"

"You are mistaken, my dear." The prince put his brandy snifter on the desk, drew her to her feet and cupped her face with his hands. "I will always need you, my dear daughter. You are as much a part of me as is Johan. You are also a reminder of your dear mother who married me as her duty to her country." He took a deep breath and smoothed May's hair. "Even though I sensed her heart was elsewhere when we married."

"Elsewhere, Papa?" She had been eleven when her mother had died tragically in a car accident. To whom was her father referring? And why was he telling her this now?

"Yes. Elena and I were betrothed almost at birth. We grew up knowing we would marry. The marriage finally took place as arranged when we were nineteen. But not before Elena gave her heart to a distant cousin."

"Who was he, Papa?"

He shook his head. "It does not matter. I only tell you this so that you understand that when the time came for your mother and me to marry, our duty came first.''

''Were you happy with Mama?'' she asked wistfully.

''Yes. We were, after all, the future prince and princess of Baronovia. Our only regret was that you were our only child. My own private regret is that I waited so long to remarry and to have another child. If I had had a son before this, you might have been spared your own arranged marriage.''

The prince walked to the window that overlooked the vast palace gardens and seemed to ponder his next words. ''Since you had never indicated you had fallen in love with someone, when it came time for you to marry, the duke was my natural choice. If only...'' His voice faded away.

''If only what, Papa?'' She went to stand at his side and took his hand.

''If only I had remembered then, as clearly as I do now, the look on your mother's face when we exchanged our marriage vows.''

May slid her arm through her father's and rested her head on his shoulder. ''What would you have done if you had remembered, Papa?''

He shrugged and kissed her forehead. ''Perhaps nothing, my dear. You had never indicated a preference for a husband, so I chose one for you. Perhaps I was wrong in my choice, but that was then and this is now. Happily I sense a second chance to put a smile on your face.''

May's heart soared as she remembered her father's earlier remark—which he had recognized she had fallen in love with Wade.

Her heart dropped just as quickly when she realized Wade was thousands of miles away and beyond her reach. She was not part of his world, nor was he part of hers. And perhaps never could be.

More to the point, had Wade actually fallen in love with her? Or, honorable man that she knew him to be, had he done his duty and moved on with his life?

''Thank you, Papa,'' she said with a catch in her throat. ''But I have no way of knowing if Commander Stevens shares the way I feel about him or that he even wishes to marry me. Perhaps I was merely part of a fairy-tale adventure.''

He patted her hand. ''We shall see, my dear. We shall see.''

SHOUTS RANG OUT, hordes of people milled around him, crushing him, pushing him out of the way, preventing from reaching the man on the stairway before it was too late.

Wade broke into a cold sweat, heard a voice cry out—his. Other voices joined his, rose in a crescendo. A woman screamed. And then, blessed silence.

Fighting off the blanket that threatened to choke him, Wade came awake, struggling to breathe. He looked around him. Thank God, he was in his own bed. The recurring dream that had tormented him for weeks began to fade and left the now-familiar uneasy feeling behind it.

Something was wrong.

He sat up in bed, threw off the blanket and set his feet on the cold floor and gradually returned to reality. Although the rerun of the night May was almost killed had been another in a series of dreams, the feeling that she needed him persisted.

He staggered into the bathroom, tore off his white T-shirt and ran cold water over his face. The doctor that had visited him in the hospital the day he had been discharged had warned him the dreams that had begun during his hospital stay would recur for a while. He had to try to remember they were only dreams and would go away in time. And that May was safely home in Baronovia.

The face that looked back at him in the bathroom mirror showed his gaunt features, shadowed eyes. If only May *had* been a dream and saving her from an assassin only a figment of an overactive imagination. The ache in his shoulder and the still-red ugly scar that ran across his chest to below his chin told the story. He and May had been closer to death than he'd realized.

He was in the process of toweling off his face and torso when the doorbell rang. Instead of being annoyed, he was actually relieved. Anything or anyone that would keep him from reliving the frightening night of the Baronovian farewell ball was welcome. Hell, if he had his way, the apartment would be wall-to-wall with people talking up a storm. Anything to bring him back into his familiar world and to make him come alive again.

As for his ever forgetting May, fat chance.

He looked through the peephole. To his surprise it was Admiral Crowley dressed in casual civilian clothing. He flung open the door. "Sir?"

The admiral strode into the room and turned around to confront Wade. "Let's call a spade a spade, Commander. I hear that you didn't pass the physical fitness exam."

It was just like his superior officer to come to the point without stopping for a hello. The only saving grace of the meeting was that Crowley was dressed in black slacks, gray shirt and a loose black corduroy jacket. A sure sign the visit obviously wasn't going to be official, but the look on the admiral's face told Wade the man meant business.

Wade ran his fingers through his still-damp hair and made for the kitchen counter. "Coffee, sir?"

"Sure," Crowley replied. He watched while Wade measured out coffee and water before he went on. "So, start at the beginning and fill me in about what's going on with you."

Wade shook his head and reached into the cupboard for two cups. "With due respect, sir, it's a long story, sir. I'm not sure you'd care to hear it."

"I wouldn't be here if I wasn't interested," Crowley answered dryly. "And on my own time, too." The scent of brewing coffee filled the air. He reached for the cup Wade handed him and took a seat at the counter. "Smells a hell of a lot better than the mud we call coffee back at my office."

A long moment passed while Wade debated how much of the true story he could tell the admiral without looking like an ass. He'd already been chewed out by Mike Wheeler for allowing May to have her way during her stay in D.C., and now he guessed it was the admiral's turn. But then, they had no way of knowing May and her determination to live like a "normal" woman while she was in D.C.

What the hell, he thought. He was already in so deep he would never climb out. What was one more chewing out? He launched into the moment Logan had told him he'd been chosen by the duchess to be her bodyguard, supposedly with the admiral's permission.

"Yeah, yeah," Crowley said impatiently. "The

State Department ran it through me first. But at the time, I sure as hell never would have believed you would wind up getting shot in the process.''

Wade went on to recount the rest of the adventurous three days with the duchess.

''You played Frisbee and danced barefoot in the grass at Georgetown Park? After the lady almost got herself kidnapped? You've got to be kidding!'' The admiral's voice and raised eyebrows registered his disbelief. But, hell, in retrospect he had a hard time believing it himself. ''Who in his right mind would have asked you to do that?''

Wade smiled at the memory of May running through the grass, her pink toes showing. And at the way she'd tied his shirt up under her breasts until she'd almost taken his breath away. ''You'd have to have known May to understand, sir. I don't think there's a man alive who could have resisted her.''

Crowley thoughtfully sipped his hot coffee. ''Had a woman like that in my life at one time.''

''How did you handle her, sir?''

''I married her.'' Crowley smiled and handed his empty cup to Wade for a refill. His mind was obviously on happy memories.

''I wasn't aware you were ever married.''

''For too short a time,'' Crowley answered in a tone that told Wade the admiral had his own mental burdens to carry. ''Now, back to you, Commander.

If you ask me, the only problems you have aren't physical. At least not enough to keep you out of the courtroom. Sounds to me as though they're mental."

Wade nodded. "Mostly at night. Asleep, I can't seem to get the shooting out of my mind. Awake, it's not much better. All I can think of is being terrified that I wouldn't reach May in time to save her."

"May? I understood the lady is Duchess Mary Louise?"

"Yes, sir. May is the name the duchess asked me to call her when we were together." Wade couldn't prevent the catch in his voice as he spoke her name. And at the memories it evoked.

Crowley stood up. "Commander, I expect to see you in my office at 0900 Monday morning ready to go back to work. In the meantime I intend to find out just what we do about those dreams of yours. For your information, no one is going to end your career except me. And I strongly advise that you don't tempt me."

Wade shut the door behind the admiral and made his way to the bathroom to shower and shave. Come hell or high water, he intended to be back on duty Monday morning or die trying. As for his nightmares, the only way his dreams would leave him in peace would be for May to come back to him.

ADMIRAL JONATHON CROWLEY, Judge Advocate General of the Department of the U.S. Navy, stared down his visitor. "Since you were the one who started the whole damn scenario, I figure you're the one to bring it to a happy conclusion."

Undersecretary of the U.S. Navy Logan, used to winding up on the short end of the stick whenever he and the admiral tangled, glared back. "I would remind you, Admiral, that it wasn't my idea. The duchess asked for Commander Stevens as an escort, and everyone agreed. Including you."

Crowley scowled and sank back in his leather chair. "To my regret, in one of my weaker moments. But why Stevens, for heaven's sake? The State Department must have been full of good-looking young men who would have fit the bill."

"Indeed," Logan sniffed. "But to hear some women tell it, none of them look like the commander when he's in full dress uniform."

Crowley grinned at the sour expression on Logan's face. "There *is* something about a uniform at that," he agreed. "Maybe you should have considered a military career for yourself."

Logan waved him off. "That's besides the point. Considering the importance of her father's visit, we were anxious to please the duchess. She specifically requested Commander Wade act as her escort. No one dreamed she could be in jeopardy."

"No?" Crowley folded his arms across his chest and raised an eyebrow. "With those countries always on the brink of some war or another, no one remembered our presence there is merely tolerated. And resented?"

Logan grimaced. "Hell, Baronovia is a mere speck on the map, important to no country but ours. Who would have dreamed some Baronovian nationalist would take it upon himself to try to assassinate the prince or his daughter to keep us out of there?"

"Your intelligence-gathering network, that's who," Crowley growled. "But that's not why I asked you to come here. Commander Stevens is in deep trouble over his handling of the duchess. Hell, I might as well come right out with it—the man damn near gave his life to save her. He sure as hell deserves some kind of reward. What are you going to do about it?"

"What would you like me to do about it?"

The admiral rose and paced the floral rug of his office. "Our new embassy is going to require the services of a legal expert. Someone well-versed in international law. Right?"

"In time, I suppose. What has that got to do with anything? Besides, if the commander is harboring any romantic illusions, I hear the lady in question is about to be remarried."

"Then I suggest you decide you need the immediate services of the commander to help staff our new embassy, Mr. Secretary,'' Crowley said as he stood over the perspiring man. ''And that you make it known to everyone, including the prince of Baronovia, that you need him on-site as soon as possible.''

Logan opened his mouth to argue the issue, then appeared to change his mind. ''And then what, Admiral?''

Crowley resumed his seat and rang for his aide. ''We allow nature to take its course. If I'm any judge of men, and I believe I am, once the commander is on-site, he can take over from there.''

Epilogue

Wade had expected there would be a price to pay for ignoring Prince Alexis's express order to stay away from his daughter, but he'd never expected anything like this.

He would have given a cheer, or at least broken out in a broad smile, if the sound of Admiral Crowley clearing his throat behind him hadn't sobered him. He squared his shoulders, stood at attention and let the show go on.

Not only had he become a believer in fairy tales, he found himself actually believing in guardian angels.

One guardian angel, incongruously enough, was his commanding officer, the grim Admiral Crowley. Crowley wasn't the type to tolerate bending regulations or the fools who broke them. And yet...

The second angel was Undersecretary of the U.S. Navy Logan. The man who had arranged Wade's current duty in the new U.S. Embassy in Baronovia. To Logan's credit, he had tried to atone for his hard-headedness by arranging to have him temporarily transferred from JAG to head up the legal section at the new U.S. Embassy.

The third angel was the ruler of Baronovia, Prince Alexis himself. A man whose written request to the State Department for Wade's presence at the new embassy apparently had crossed the Atlantic at the same time Logan was submitting Wade's credentials for approval.

The miracle was that although these three men had little in common, they had gotten their act together long enough to accomplish it.

Wade pulled his thoughts together in time to hear the tail end of the prince's speech.

"And so, Commander Wade Stevens, I hereby grant you knighthood and the honorary title of Duke of Baronovia."

With those final words, the prince hung a ribbon around Wade's neck and kissed him on both cheeks and walked up the aisle to escort the bride.

Wade finally allowed himself to smile. This was a heck of a beginning for a wedding, but he'd be the last man on earth to complain.

Not when he was about to marry May, the woman of his heart. And not when being created a duke meant he and his bride would be able to start their life together on an equal footing.

He would need all the status he could acquire, honorary or not, to convince his bride to let him make the rules when they got home to D.C.

His mouth became suddenly dry and his nerves quivered at the realization he was actually about to marry his May in her fairy-tale country of Baronovia. A country that seemed to be right out of the old Mario Lanza movie, *The Student Prince.*

Outside the palace, the last time he'd looked, the entire tiny country waited for the ceremony to be over and the celebrating to begin. Trimmed hedges were covered with balloons and streamers. Water fountains had been decorated with fresh flowers. Costumed palace servants were setting out platters high with food on trestle tables. Costumed musicians were warming up on a platform on a manicured lawn.

He settled the sword that hung at the waist of his dress uniform and waited for the ceremony to begin.

A flurry of trumpets sounded. The string orchestra, hidden behind foliage in a balcony, struck up a wedding march. At the end of the ballroom, the wide doors opened and two flower girls carrying baskets filled with rose petals appeared. Trying hard not to giggle, the two little girls started down the aisle tossing petals in their wake.

Ten bridesmaids, all relatives of the duchess and clad in dresses clearly intended to resemble Baronovia's national costume, made their way down the aisle in the center of the room. After a pause, there was another flurry of trumpets and the bride appeared.

Wade's heart almost took flight at the sight of his bride coming down the aisle on her father's arm. There was nothing old-fashioned about her. She wore a simple, long, white silk Vera Wang gown, bare at her silken shoulders and ending at her ankles, where pink manicured toenails were shod in white satin sandals. Instead of the diamond tiara she'd worn the last time he'd seen her, a wreath of pink baby roses nestled in her hair. A simple gold chain hung around her neck.

There was no mistaking the meaning of the simplicity of both her wedding gown and her jewelry. Nor the loving glow in her exotic green eyes and the smile that curved at her lips.

In her own way, May was signaling him she was no longer Duchess Mary Louise of Lorrania. She was the woman who had fallen in love with "American" food, enjoyed chocolate sundaes, had thrown Frisbees and danced barefoot in the grass in his arms.

When they approached the altar and May's eyes met his, any doubts Wade might have had that she was ready to trade her royal title for the life of a typical American woman faded.

Typical be damned, he thought with a broad smile. This was his May. There was nothing typical about her, thank God.

The prince handed his daughter to the groom, bowed briefly and stepped aside.

Somewhere in the audience women sobbed. Men cleared their throats. The minister stepped forward and the music stopped.

Wade took May's hand in his, kissed her wrist and gazed down into her eyes. "I love you," he whispered.

"I love you, too," she said as he took her hand, tucked it in his arm and led her to the flower-covered altar. "Forever."

* * * * *

Beginning in October from

HARLEQUIN®

AMERICAN *Romance*®

TRADING PLACES

A brand-new duo from
popular Harlequin authors

RITA HERRON
and
DEBRA WEBB

When identical twin brothers decide to trade lives,
they get much more than they bargained for!

Available October 2002

THE RANCHER WORE SUITS
by Rita Herron
Rugged rancher Ty Cooper uses his down-home
charms to woo beautiful pediatrician Jessica.

Available November 2002

THE DOCTOR WORE BOOTS
by Debra Webb
Ty's next-door neighbor Leanne finds herself falling for
sophisticated and sexy Dr. Dex Montgomery.

Available at your favorite retail outlet.

HARLEQUIN®
Makes any time special ®

Princes...Princesses...
London Castles...New York Mansions...
To live the life of a royal!

**In 2002, Harlequin Books lets you escape to a
world of royalty with these royally themed titles:**

Temptation:
January 2002—*A Prince of a Guy* (#861)
February 2002—*A Noble Pursuit* (#865)

American Romance:
The Carradignes: American Royalty (Editorially linked series)
March 2002—*The Improperly Pregnant Princess* (#913)
April 2002—*The Unlawfully Wedded Princess* (#917)
May 2002—*The Simply Scandalous Princess* (#921)
November 2002—*The Inconveniently Engaged Prince* (#945)

Intrigue:
The Carradignes: A Royal Mystery (Editorially linked series)
June 2002—*The Duke's Covert Mission* (#666)

Chicago Confidential
September 2002—*Prince Under Cover* (#678)

The Crown Affair
October 2002—*Royal Target* (#682)
November 2002—*Royal Ransom* (#686)
December 2002—*Royal Pursuit* (#690)

Harlequin Romance:
June 2002—*His Majesty's Marriage* (#3703)
July 2002—*The Prince's Proposal* (#3709)

Harlequin Presents:
August 2002—*Society Weddings* (#2268)
September 2002—*The Prince's Pleasure* (#2274)

Duets:
September 2002—*Once Upon a Tiara/Henry Ever After* (#83)
October 2002—*Natalia's Story/Andrea's Story* (#85)

Celebrate a year of royalty with
Harlequin Books!

Available at your favorite retail outlet.

HARLEQUIN®
Makes any time special®

Visit us at www.eHarlequin.com

HSROY02

If you enjoyed what you just read,
then we've got an offer you can't resist!

Take 2 bestselling
love stories FREE!

Plus get a FREE surprise gift!

Clip this page and mail it to Harlequin Reader Service®

IN U.S.A.	**IN CANADA**
3010 Walden Ave.	P.O. Box 609
P.O. Box 1867	Fort Erie, Ontario
Buffalo, N.Y. 14240-1867	L2A 5X3

YES! Please send me 2 free Harlequin American Romance® novels and my free surprise gift. After receiving them, if I don't wish to receive anymore, I can return the shipping statement marked cancel. If I don't cancel, I will receive 4 brand-new novels every month, before they're available in stores! In the U.S.A., bill me at the bargain price of $3.99 plus 25¢ shipping & handling per book and applicable sales tax, if any*. In Canada, bill me at the bargain price of $4.74 plus 25¢ shipping & handling per book and applicable taxes**. That's the complete price and a savings of at least 10% off the cover prices—what a great deal! I understand that accepting the 2 free books and gift places me under no obligation ever to buy any books. I can always return a shipment and cancel at any time. Even if I never buy another book from Harlequin, the 2 free books and gift are mine to keep forever.

154 HDN DNT7
354 HDN DNT9

Name	(PLEASE PRINT)	
Address	Apt.#	
City	State/Prov.	Zip/Postal Code

* Terms and prices subject to change without notice. Sales tax applicable in N.Y.
** Canadian residents will be charged applicable provincial taxes and GST.
  All orders subject to approval. Offer limited to one per household and not valid to
  current Harlequin American Romance® subscribers.
  ® are registered trademarks of Harlequin Enterprises Limited.

AMER02   ©2001 Harlequin Enterprises Limited

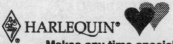

Say "I do" with

HARLEQUIN®

AMERICAN *Romance*®

and

Kara Lennox

How to Marry A HARDISON

**First you tempt him. Then you tame him...
all the way to the altar.**

PLAIN JANE'S PLAN
October 2002

Plain Jane Allison Crane knew her chance had finally
come to catch the eye of her lifelong crush, Jeff Hardison.
With a little help from a friend—and one great big
makeover—could Allison finally win her heart's desire?

Don't miss the other titles in this series:

VIXEN IN DISGUISE
August 2002

SASSY CINDERELLA
December 2002

HARLEQUIN®
Makes any time special ®

Visit us at www.eHarlequin.com   HARHTMAH2